Stories by

THE LITTLE
RESTAURANT

This book is edited and designed by the Editorial Committee of
Cultural China series

Managing Directors: Wang Youbu, Xu Naiqing
Editorial Director: Wu Ying
Series Editor: Wang Jiren
Editor: Nina Train Choa

Text by Wang Anyi
Translation by Yawtsong Lee

Interior and Cover Design: Wang Wei
Cover Image: Getty Images

ISBN: 978-1-60220-225-2

Address any comments about *The Little Restaurant* to:

Better Link Press
99 Park Ave
New York, NY 10016
USA
or
Shanghai Press and Publishing Development Company
F 7 Donghu Road, Shanghai, China (200031)
Email: comments_betterlinkpress@hotmail.com

Printed in China by Shanghai Donnelley Printing Co. Ltd.

1 2 3 4 5 6 7 8 9 10

THE LITTLE RESTAURANT

By Wang Anyi

Better Link Press

Preface

English readers will be presented with a set of 12 pocket books. These books contain outstanding novellas written by 12 writers from Shanghai over the past 30 years. Most of the writers were born in Shanghai from the late 1940's to the late 1950's. They started their literary careers during or after the 1980's. For various reasons, most of them lived and worked in the lowest social strata in other cities or in rural areas for much of their adult lives. As a result they saw much of the world and learned lessons from real life before finally returning to Shanghai. They embarked on their literary careers for various reasons, but most of them were simply passionate about writing. The writers are involved in a variety of occupations, including university professors, literary editors, leaders of literary institutions and professional writers. The diversity of topics covered in these novellas will lead readers to discover the different experiences and motivations of the authors. Readers will encounter a fascinating range of esthetic convictions as they analyze the authors' distinctive artistic skills and writing styles. Generally speaking, a realistic writing style dominates most of their literary works. The literary works they have elaborately created are a true reflection of drastic social changes, as well as differing perspectives towards urban life in Shanghai. Some works created by avant-garde writers have been selected in order to present a variety of styles. No matter what writing styles they adopt though, these writers have enjoyed a definite place, and exerted a positive influence, in Chinese literary circles over the past three decades.

Known as the "Paris of the Orient" around the world, Shanghai was already an international metropolis in the 1920's and 1930's. During that period, Shanghai was China's economic, cultural and literary center. A high number of famous Chinese writers lived, created and published their literary works in Shanghai, including, Lu Xun, Guo Moruo, Mao Dun and Ba Jin. Today, Shanghai has become a globalized metropolis. Writers who have pursued a literary career in the past 30 years are now faced with new challenges and opportunities. I am confident that some of them will produce other fine and influential literary works in the future. I want to make it clear that this set of pocket books does not include all representative Shanghai writers. When the time is ripe, we will introduce more representative writers to readers in the English-speaking world.

Wang Jiren
Series Editor

Contents

The Little Restaurant

If you walk by this little restaurant in a makeshift building and poke your head through the door for a look inside, you'd think, "How can people live like this?" It's not so much disapproval, nor certainly approval, as a paralysis of judgment or some incomprehension on your part that prompts the question: "How can people live like this?"

The little restaurant is situated in a busy, noisy alley leading, at either end, into major arteries heavily traveled by motor vehicles, a lot of which are diverted through the alley. The pedestrians also treat it as a thoroughfare, perhaps more so than cars. In fact the alley has all the characteristics of a thoroughfare: It has a decent width and sub-alleys as cross streets. It even boasts an upper sidewalk and a lower sidewalk. The fact that it has not been designated as a street is probably due to an oversight in municipal government. As a result it has been given a number, which is attached to the word "Alley," in the same way the other alleys abutting the street at one end and all the houses on that street are numbered. It is not a distinguished alley. Illustrious alleys are known for their distinctive architectural styles, whereas this alley is an architectural patchwork. There used to be some small and medium-sized factories and a school, interspersed with residential buildings, mostly shanties and a few two-story structures of brick and wood construction that could, only by a stretch of the imagination, be called Western-style houses. This architectural jumble in the alley is rather more characteristic of a street. Undoubtedly it was once a quiet lane with negligible traffic, human or vehicular. A section of a high wall still left standing today evokes the picture of a little frequented alley in bygone days: concrete utility poles standing outside the whitewashed wall, at one end of which hung a street lamp with a galvanized shade. The shanties, crowded and noisy, were set way back from the alley in a warren of back alleys, while the main alley itself remained free of bustle and stir, its pebble pavement below the concrete upper sidewalk kept very clean.

But now all that has changed. The shanties were razed, replaced by new public housing projects. Developers bought up land underneath bankrupt factories and built private apartment buildings on it. The school was moved elsewhere. The buildings now lining the alley all went up in the last two decades and more are in the pipeline. Each project was planned independently, with no thought given to compatibility and

harmony with surrounding structures. The
result is a disorganized jumble of disparate
buildings, with a bewildering assortment of
orientations, heights and ages. The messy
construction sites sandwiched between the
finished projects are a veritable eyesore.
In order to generate revenue and to create
livelihoods for its unemployed residents, the
local community has built on the previous
upper sidewalks two rows of makeshift
buildings partitioned into storefronts rented
out to laid-off neighborhood workers, most
of whom would sublease the storefronts to
migrant workers, at a markup, pocketing the
difference. They would then go elsewhere
to make easier money. The migrant workers
come in families, with at least two kids in
each household. The two or three square
meters of store space serve as storefront
during the day and bedroom at night.
Cooking, washing and eating are done at
the curb. They throw household waste water
and trash into the street, ever faithful to
their custom and tradition in their village

of origin. They let their children run free in the alley as they'd put their sheep out to pasture down on the farm. The kids weave between cars and people, with no sense of the dangers lurking everywhere. In the local sections of the evening papers, one reads news stories about children falling into manholes or kidnapped by human traffickers. A majority of these incidents happen in alleys such as this one and involve migrant children.

In the alley where the little restaurant is located, the businesses run by out-of-towners fall under the following categories. One such category is retail stores selling building and home furnishing materials, run in the majority of cases by migrants from Fujian Province, whose possible links with the string of lumber yards lining the major street outside the alley, run by folks from Nanping of Fujian, are to be confirmed. These retail businesses sell cement, sand, bricks, paints, glues and door locks, hinges, handles and curtain rods. These home furnishing products look no different from those sold in major stores, but their prices are often one tenth of those charged by the latter. For example a hinge may cost over a hundred yuan in a home furnishings superstore but you can get it here for only 12 yuan. And there are volume discounts. They are pretty open about these products being counterfeits, but on the other hand, they say, who can vouch for the authenticity of the more expensive 100-yuan items? Both versions do the job they are supposed to do, so why be a sucker and pay an exorbitant price for the expensive equivalent of a much cheaper version? This is their standard pitch to potential customers. They also have an ability to establish a quick rapport with the construction crews, composed mostly of migrant workers, who work on the building sites in the neighborhood. Theirs is clearly a mutually beneficial relationship, with some construction workers buying supplies regularly at a certain store, where they get invoices, whose truthfulness is privileged information between buyer and seller, for subsequent reimbursements from their employers. If their employer happens to be one who insists on personally scrutinizing every little expense, the construction crew members would artificially raise the budget estimates and return some merchandise for cash after the procurement. Such deals are conducted semi-openly and are difficult to police. These Fujian migrants are typically short in stature and energetic, with dark complexions, high brows and sunken eyes. Their eyes are alert and observant at all times. They appear to possess both brain and brawn. Among themselves they speak an extremely esoteric Fujian dialect with a harsh-, even agitated-sounding tone. When it is necessary to speak Mandarin with people not from their part of the country, a stubborn Fujian accent makes their speech appear a little halting; but it is no barrier to effective communication. As a matter of fact they communicate rather more effectively than others, because their accent conveys a certainty and finality that helps them put their point across.

Besides building materials, another business favored by would-be migrant entrepreneurs is that of food stalls.

Ownership in the business of food stalls is less uniform. Some may advertise Lanzhou *lamian* (hand-pulled noodles from Lanzhou City) although the owner may not hail from Lanzhou but from Shandong Province having maybe learned the trade from a Lanzhou native. Or the owner simply capitalizes on the fame of Lanzhou lamian to sell an entirely different sort of hand-pulled noodles. Besides migrants from Shandong, there are food purveyors from the central region of Anhui Province, the north region of Jiangsu Province and Zhejiang Province. For breakfast they uniformly offer soy milk, fried crullers and glutinous rice balls; for lunch and supper they offer sautéed dishes, noodles and combination platters. These are businesses that require hard work. The owners never have a moment of rest; before the breakfast shift is over, they already start sorting vegetables, mincing meat, rinsing rice and laying out the various meat and vegan dishes for patrons to choose from. The meat dishes normally include pot-stewed eggs, pork spareribs, braised pork chops, meatballs, deep-fried sole and smoked mackerel. The vegetable dishes are kelp knots, spicy Ma Po Tofu, bean sprouts and seasonal vegetables. After storing the already prepared dishes in large enamel containers and aluminum trays in the store, the owners immediately start preparing the ingredients for à la carte dishes. The bloodied and dirty water from rinsing the meat and vegetables and cleaning the fish runs off into the culverts, often overflowing the sluggish gutters and flooding the pavement, covering it with vegetable leaves and fish scale that attract swarms of flies. Cats from neighboring stores come rummaging for food around the table and chair legs, hauling the fish innards about and freely scattering fleas

and lice. By midday the cart with a wide
selection of prepared dishes will have been
wheeled out to the edge of the sidewalk and
the ingredients for à la carte dishes readied
and spread out. The store will be busy until
about two in the afternoon when they get
some rest during a lull in business. The
owners and hired help would sit or stand
in front of the store doing a bit of people-
gazing or visit other stores for a chat. The
girls hired by the restaurants, dressed in
bright colors, their synthetic fiber blouses
trimmed at the neck and cuffs with broad
bands of lace bearing intricate water lily
leaf patterns and wearing plastic slippers
on their feet, may or may not have come
from the same village as the store owners.
They may have traveled from as far as
Sichuan or Hubei Province. Prolonged
exposure to intense ultraviolet radiation
has left on their cheeks two large, deep
blushes that make their eyes look small and
lusterless, giving these girls a falsely dull
look. They are certainly more guileless by

far than the girls working in the equally numerous hair salons, whose eyes always have a sparkle—sometimes a suggestive look—in them. Their job consists mainly of hair-washing and massages. They stand behind the customer, their hands kneading and massaging the scalp topped by a pile of snow-white suds. When they hear someone pass outside the door, they slightly tilt their head sideways to size up the subject out of the corner of their eyes in a cool detached look that at the same time seems to beckon warmly. The gold earrings on their earlobes swing and bob in step with the kneading motions, giving off a bright golden gleam. All their gold jewelry appears without exception to be high in gold content and bright yellow in color, a symbol of their higher income and status. At nightfall when most other businesses have shuttered their stores and extinguished their lights, the hair salons remain brightly illuminated by high-lumen florescent fixtures, a beehive of activity and banter, highlighted by the surrounding quiet along the length of the street. But for this activity, the street would have been scarcely different from a country lane. It is the salons that give it the semblance of a city street and bring night life to the neighborhood. At these hours taxis or private cars drive through the alley discreetly, carrying residents back to the newly constructed apartments; these are people who have a night life. Vehicular traffic occasionally gets quite heavy; the cars driving in opposite directions acknowledge each other by flickering their headlights on and off, but without honking. In these hours, everything is done discreetly. One day a male voice erupted in a hair salon, hurling vitriolic abuse in the foulest local language, his curses reverberating along the length of the alley, but the vehicular traffic moved along as if nothing had happened and the quiet of the street remained undisturbed.

These are the main businesses lining the alley. Then there are the purveyors of teas from Mount Huangshan of Anhui, tailors from Ningbo of Zhejiang and shoe repairmen from Haimen. You'll also find stores specializing in wreaths and other funeral articles, appliance repair service, foodstuffs and housewares, makers of steel doors, glaziers, marble craftsmen, bicycle repairs, etc. In the morning the street comes alive with a symphony—or cacophony—of the sounds of the radio turned on by the tailor busying himself with dressmaking and alterations, the channel-surfing by the appliance repairman on the TV he is working on, the steel door maker cutting steel with his torch and the electric grinder of the marble craftsman. The alley is then truly full of effervescence. Its denizens, having converged in this little street from all across the country, have come to know each other and become friends, especially next door neighbors, who share plumbing and electricity and help each other to clean up the front of the stores in preparation for visits and inspections by the Bureau of Industry and Commerce and the sanitation department. They also cover for next door storekeepers who have temporarily stepped out and take care of their customers and negotiate prices in their absence. Their children also hang out and play in the street together. Solidarity is indispensable for these migrants who have come from far away to this huge, unfamiliar city, whose riffraff will inevitably bully the outsiders. The riffraff of the city, while held in contempt by the locals, flaunt their city credentials to intimidate and milk the out-of-towners. They normally do this by obtaining goods and services without paying for them, or by extorting money on the pretext that standards and regulations have not been complied with. These villagers are mostly unsophisticated, simple folks who are easily intimidated because they are often predisposed to self-blame. The more defiant ones invariably find their attempt to stand up to the bullies unprofitable. This is, after all, the locals' turf and they can muster an "army" at a moment's notice. The migrants therefore also need to band together so that whenever there's a dispute, they too can come out in force, not to get into a physical fight but to mediate, offer support, take sides, or take the sting out of the dispute. It's to their advantage not to antagonize the locals, if only because harmony breeds profit, as merchants like to say. They have to take it under the chin in order to gain a toehold here, no matter how rotten they feel inside.

On the surface the businesses on this little street operate independently of each other but the truth is they are organized into cohesive guilds that deter unauthorized price-cutting. With prices fixed by the trade organizations, the only room for maneuver is found in the quality and quantity of merchandise. Cheating is collective and orchestrated. Solidarity pervades the alley. A walk from one end of the little street to the other will generate in you a growing, eerie sense of being in a forbidding fortress. You feel eyes sizing you up, photographing and storing you face pixel by pixel, and piecing together your life, movements and relationships. Not one of those living in the housing projects or the new apartment buildings could escape being ensnared in this web of visual inspection. The residents in the new apartment buildings, who often lead a more secluded life, become a prized quarry for the hunting eyes. When these residents address them, they are often flustered, as if unable to disengage themselves quickly enough from this close scrutiny of the community. They hasten to put on a smile, which takes on an obsequious tint because of the haste in its formation. They become verbose as they dance attendance on these shoppers. The unheralded skirmish momentarily throws them off balance and embarrasses them. But the moment the shoppers leave, they recover their cool and the sharp eagle-eyed look returns.

Besides the stores, peddlers ply their trade in the alley. These are people who lay out their wares on the sidewalk in the morning—home-made shirts and pajamas, shoes and hosiery items sourced from liquidated factories at bargain basement prices—and stay until about eight or nine. There are salesmen pitching their chili powder, MSG and other spices to restaurants, and those who peddle shampoos and cosmetic products to hair salons. These salespeople, notably those selling to the hair salons, are well-dressed and carry attaché cases containing their samples. After a while they've made friends here and when they visit they often sit for long chats about everything and nothing. They are gregarious types believing that one of the nice things about having friends is that they always invite you to their table. In some sense they consider friends a meal ticket and therefore are not stingy with the time spent on cultivating friendships. A Cantonese man selling chinaware is a frequent caller. He still sells his wares the simple, old way, with bowls and plates stacked in bamboo baskets that dangle at two ends of a bamboo pole slung over his shoulder. The bowls and plates are stamped on their bottoms with the brand name "Jingdezhen," the town famous for its porcelain ware. These are undoubtedly irregular, defective, botched products from Jingdezhen kilns because for one thing the bowls are not perfectly round. On the other hand you pay a very low price for them and if you drive a hard bargain you can bring the price down even further. He comes here almost daily, picks an eatery where he has his bowl of noodles, leaving his baskets at the curb. He will come out of the restaurant the moment someone shows an interest in his wares. In short, business is brisk on this street.

The alley is a haven for migrant workers. They feel at home here. They are familiar with all the different kinds of shops and stores, some run by folks from their native villages and others not. It makes no difference to them because somehow they can find a distant blood link. Most of these migrants are construction workers on nearby construction sites or do home furnishing projects in the new apartments. After work they would come here in the evening in groups, flirting with the girls from the hair salons, joining bull sessions at store counters or having a few drinks over sautéed dishes ordered at a small restaurant. These are the best hours of the day for small eateries. Under the illumination of 200-lumen bulbs the kitchen crackles with multi-colored ingredients being stirred and tossed in the woks, then ladled as greasy finished products into containers. A festive mood floats in the air, with beers frothing and the patrons boisterously playing drinkers' games of finger-guessing and wagering. Unable to hold the large amounts of beer they've consumed, the drinkers would find a corner in the alley to relieve themselves openly and unabashedly, sometimes even engaging someone in small talk with their fly open. This street is chock

full of delights but is no stranger to filth
and seediness. Nobody takes it seriously or
has any sense of shame when they indulge
in their peccadilloes here. As some would
say, they've got nothing to lose anyway.
Even ordinarily well-behaved chaps no
longer care about "face" once they are here.
Their permissive and open mores does
not arise from an emancipated mind but
rather reflect a mentality that sees nothing
wrong with doing further damage to what
is already damaged. Nothing illustrates this
mentality better than the phenomenon of
people relieving themselves wherever they
feel the need. More beer into their bellies
invariably leads to bigger trouble, which
will start with verbal abuse in their shared
dialect, followed by fisticuffs, which will be
a signal for the restaurant owner to chase the
whole lot of them into the street and shutter
the place. With so much construction going
on in the neighborhood, there is a plentiful
supply of bricks and sand, which become
handy missiles for them to hurl at each

other. The girls working in the hair salons might watch the pitched battle from behind the glass doors but none of them would dial the emergency 110 number. The warriors will disperse at the sound of the motorcycles of police patrolmen who happen by. And quiet returns to the little street.

This is a typical picture of the daily goings-on in the alley.

The little restaurant in question is situated near one end of the alley. It takes up the space of three or four makeshift storefronts, whose partition walls have been knocked down for the purpose of accommodating the eatery. The "little" restaurant is a bit of a misnomer because it boasts after all the biggest store space in the entire alley. It has an asphalt felt roof topped by an extra layer of fiberglass and whitewashed single-brick-width walls. The doors and windows were cannibalized from some abandoned or condemned building; the vintage double wooden doors can't even close properly because of sloppy

installation. The windows are also visibly
out of plumb. The place bears a close
physical resemblance to a roadside food
stall catering to motorists on the highways,
and I don't mean a roadside food stall in the
south but one commonly found in the more
desolate parts of north China. Whenever
a motor vehicle approaches, a colorfully
dressed young woman steps out from the
eatery and waves the motorists to a stop
inviting their patronage. The whitewashed
walls, the wooden door in a grievous state,
the rusted steel window bars, the grimy
window panes, the stains of waste water
marring the pavement in front and the
strong odors of onions, ginger, grease and
sauces wafting out of the door of this little
restaurant in the alley are typical of its crude,
filthy and forlorn northern cousins without
their generous and solid feel. Its walls are
flimsy, as is its roof, and its foundation is
clearly far from solid. The walls have been
blackened at the base by mold and rot
fostered by the damp southern air. Instead

of the wholesome smoky smell of the north, it gives off a cloying, sickly sweet odor, as if a dead cat or a dead rat lies hidden somewhere. In short it has a run-down look, lacking any appeal or flair. There appears to be nothing to look forward to and nothing that would induce a potential customer to venture in.

But this pessimistic prognosis is belied by the fact that it is doing a decent business. Like the other eateries in the alley, it also offers combination platters, but on a different scale. Not too far away across the street is a stock brokerage firm run by out-of-towners. The individual, small-time traders conducting their transactions there get their boxed lunches in the little restaurant, which also gets patronage from people working for a glue manufacturer, an office of some sort and a real estate agency nearby. So it is doing a brisk business, which becomes hectic and overwhelming at noon time, when girls hired as temporary help take out large plastic bags containing piles of takeout orders of boxed lunches and go off in all directions to deliver them. When individual patrons come in to order their lunch, the owner would often take the order himself. He holds the plastic lunch container in front of his chest with his deformed, curled hand and ladles food with the other hand into the container. Every time he has to raise the ladle up to the level of his chin in order to get the food into the container. A cigarette dangles from a corner of his mouth, its long ashy tip in perpetual danger of falling into the container. The food itself does not look particularly appetizing; meatballs made dark and shiny by an overabundance of corn starch and soy sauce; spareribs awash in a thick paste; wilted cabbage leaves; hard segments of bean curd skin that should have been soaked and softened first. Vegetables that are supposed to be sautéed without sauce, cucumbers that are supposed to be prepared as a tossed salad and fish that is supposed to be deep-fried often come out

colored by the dark sauce dripping from
the ladle. Even the limp notes of change
given back to the customers are stained and
made sticky by the dark sauce. Yet none of
that affects its booming business. Besides
takeout orders of boxed lunches, it also
boasts a decent eat-in crowd, occupying
about 60 percent of its dozen tables. These
are people who come for noodles or à la
carte dishes.

As in a roadside food stall, its rectangular,
bare wood tables arranged classroom-style
in two rows are covered by disposable sheets
of plastic film and the chairs are round
stools with vinyl seats and steel legs. The
tables and the stools wobble like seesaws,
because of the unevenness either of their
legs or of the floor, which is made of vinyl
printed with a lattice pattern of alternating
black and white squares. The vinyl flooring
must have been laid directly over concrete
and you could feel its coldness even through
the soles of your shoes. The quality of the
vinyl flooring is such that it is very easy

to soil but very hard to clean and with use
both the white and the black squares have
turned gray and the floor is oil-stained
and pockmarked with cigarette burns.
The walls are covered by vinyl low-foam
wallpaper that likewise is easy to dirty and
hard to clean and has yellowed with time.
It has peeled off in places and dark lines
have formed along the seams incrusted
with grime. All this is charitably covered
up under dim light. But on days of bright
sunshine, the swirling dust particles in the
air are revealed in revolting detail. The
unsparing light of the sun's rays highlight
the pockmarked surfaces of the floor and
the walls, with all the seaminess and squalor
in plain sight. Keeping the light too dim
confers no advantage either, because when
someone turns on the light—and florescent
light at that—the extra brightness will put in
sharp relief the stains and scars, including
the grease and splotches on people's faces
and add a greenish sheen to the faces. The
owner, whose face is already not much to

look at, now looks positively ghoulish with bulging veins on his temples.

It is a mystery that the little restaurant is doing so well under the circumstances. Maybe people nowadays no longer much mind filth. Those small-time speculators spending their days in the stock brokerage across the street may not be volume traders but they are smartly dressed in suits and all have a cell phone in their hand. Yet they don't feel embarrassed to order boxed lunches at the little restaurant; nor do they mind the owner holding the lunch box with his deformed, curled hand and the cigarette dangling above it threatening to spice up the lunch with the trembling ash. Outside the small restaurant, the trader behaves like a decent, civil man, but once he steps into the restaurant, he sheds his manners and starts spitting, flicking cigarette ash wherever he chooses, and chewing food with a loud, smacking sound and slurping his noodles noisily. He unbuttons his suit but is careful to keep his elbows suspended to avoid staining his sleeves and cuffs. In a place filled with grease and sauces, he has the enviable ability to keep his clothes clean and his hair in perfect shape, so that he walks out in exactly the same pristine state as when he walked in. He may eat a boxed lunch or a bowl of noodles in this little restaurant at noon time; that is not to say he will not be seen feasting on a live lobster in some upscale seafood restaurant in the evening. But even then he will keep his elbows suspended as he wields his chopsticks, a habit developed in his patronage of the little restaurant. He has an exemplary faculty for feeling comfortable both in an elevated position and in a lowly station.

The owner of the little restaurant is a local Shanghainese. Judging from the name "Little Restaurant" which he has devised for it, the owner appears to be cultured to have thought of such a fine name that embodies the principle: "There is elegance in simplicity." It's hard to guess his age.

He appears to be in his 40s, probably someone in the generation of the *laosanjie* ("old three classes," those who were in secondary school in 1966 when the Cultural Revolution erupted). But then he may very well be in his early 30s because people age faster in this kind of unclean environment. You can never tell though. This kind of life can retard aging; it may freeze time and age. So it is really hard to make an educated guess about the owner's age. He is very thin; his skin tightly drawn over his cheekbones and his cheeks, so much so that his eyes appear to protrude. The curious lack of wrinkles on his face makes his age an even greater mystery. The lack of wrinkles hasn't however made him any younger-looking. At first blush, his face appears unclean, with seeming stains on his eyelids, the hollows of his nose, his jowls and his forehead. Upon closer scrutiny, the stains prove nonexistent. He has sparse eyebrows and thinning hair, strands of which stick close to the scalp probably because of the dampness from the

grease and fumes of cooking he is constantly
exposed to. He has large, flat hands that
are of a light-complexion and, though not
coarse, seem to speak of a hard life, not in a
physical sense but in the sense of being dealt
a lousy card by life. Most of the time he is
seen sitting at a square table by the door.
On the table is a wooden case with a double
lid that is hinged in the middle so that its
two leafs can be independently lifted. It is
his cash box and he handles all the cash.
The limp, soiled, damp change comes out
of this box. When the owner receives cash
from customers and gives change, he yells at
the girls hired as temps, who are preparing
takeout orders or bussing trays. His voice
is loud but not stern and the migrant girls,
clearly unimpressed, continue to drag their
feet and take their time.

The girls who work in the little restaurant
are all under 20, as are most other girls
working in the food stalls dotting the alley,
and do the same kind of work for a living,
yet they appear more hard-boiled, unlike

the girls in other, smaller food stalls, who are more solicitous and hardworking, and are quick to reel off to the customer the prices of different combinations: so much for one meat dish and two veggie dishes, so much for two meat dishes and one veggie and so much for two meat and two veggie dishes. When they sense hesitation or indecision, they will make suggestions and recommendations. They speak Mandarin or the local Shanghainese dialect with a thick accent; their faces are fresh and flushed. Their hands, though chapped from long immersion in brine and greasy water, are otherwise healthy, strong and deft. They fill the lunch box with food, secure the lid, put it in a plastic bag and slip in a pair of disposable chopsticks before handing it reverentially to the customer. This reverence to the value of food and all other bounties of nature is only observable in people who have worked the land. They may give you less rice than you'd expect out of an instinct of stinginess but it will still be enough for you. When they ladle the food into the box, they would appear to be more generous but in fact they have perfect control over the amount doled out. They maintain the same reverential air when they fill the lunch boxes with food. They've retained their innocence, still unspoiled by life in the city or in the alley.

The girls working in the "Little Restaurant" are a breed apart. They seem to have an aversion to talking, as if speech took too much out of them. When pressed hard, they will throw an impatient, rapid-fire reply at you in a heavily accented Mandarin or Shanghainese. The words slip off their tongues unctuously, in a matter reminiscent of the glibness of old-timers of Beijing, slurred over and often unintelligible. But the fear of being rebuffed discourages you from further attempts at seeking clarification. When you examine the food exhibited in the containers and try to decide which ones to pick, they will look into the air with their heads tilted up and sideways, while drumming the enamel containers with the ladle in their hand. When you have pointed at one meat dish and one veggie and are having a hard time deciding on what else to choose, they would quickly close the lid on the lunch box and pass the box along with a pair of disposable chopsticks out of the window in the glass partition. It should have been mentioned that the takeout boxed lunches at "The Little Restaurant" are sold from behind a glass partition, which separates the boxed lunches placed on an inside counter and the *xiaojie* ("miss") handling them from the customer on the outside. By the way, these girls should be called *xiaojie*; the glass partition raises the status of the boxed lunches and the *xiaojie*. Obviously the flies continue their mid-air minuets despite the fancy partition. When after much hesitation you've made one meat and one veggie choice and are hard pressed to name one more choice, the *xiaojie* slaps the lunch box shut, demands payment and sends you on your way. Just as you are on the point of leaving submissively, a customer behind you on the line reminds you that you are entitled to one more choice of vegetables, to make up the minimum one meat and two vegetables combination. So you remonstrate with the miss who sold you the lunch. This unleashes a torrent of a reply to the effect that you passed on a third pick; I told you in no uncertain terms that it's five yuan for one meat two veggies, six yuan for two meat one veggie and seven yuan for two meat and two veggie picks. You passed on a third pick. I couldn't very well force it on you. There is no refund for food you declined of your own accord. As she rapidly moves her lips and flips her eyes, you risk being drowned in her torrent of words. Were it not for her native accent tripping up her tongue, handicapping her verbal delivery, she would be speaking a perfect version of the city's singsong dialect. But her style is not that far from the way of the snobbish salesgirls in the city's department stores, who are famous for an unsparing tongue. What they lack is the city girls' subtlety and so they often appear rude and their words and gestures exaggerated. Sometimes when you forget to mention it's for takeout and not eat-in, and they are too lazy to ask, they more or less deliberately use a lidless lunch box to hold the lunch you've ordered, making it impossible for you to take it with you. If you tell her it's a takeout order, she will not refill the order with a lidded container but will simply put another lidless one over the order and press it back into your hand. If you dare to remonstrate further, you'll be deluged by another torrent of words. They are not above shortchanging you in the amount of food ladled into your container, sometimes to the point of absurdity. For instance if you pick kelp knots, she will give you two, and if you order fried bean curd, she gives you three pieces, not out of stinginess but as a form of harassment and a power play meant to tell you she has control over the amount she decides to mete out to you and there's little you can do about it.

But the Little Restaurant is doing a thriving business despite all that. What can you say?

The Little Restaurant does not sell breakfasts. That gives it the status of a regular restaurant. It opens for business about 10 a.m., when the door and the windows are opened and the drapes over the display window parted. At this early hour the display window still shows the previous day's dishes. These won't be replaced with the day's fresh prepared dishes until about 11 a.m. but it's anybody's guess whether the fresh preparations are mixed with the previous day's fare because no one has witnessed the changing of the dishes. The owner sits in his usual spot at the square table by the door guarding his cash box. The girls sweep the floor and wipe off the tables. The place has been spruced up a bit of late, so there is a sort of a fresh look. The sun, by now high in the sky, brightens up half of the interior of the restaurant. As mentioned previously, this restaurant does not bear up to scrutiny under bright illumination, which brings out the tired look. As a consequence what little freshness there is disappears instantly. The greenish sheen on the owner's face turns sicklier, as if he had stayed up late and hadn't had sufficient sleep. The girls, on the other hand, are fresh and alive on account of their youth and still warm and dry from a good night's sleep under their comfortable quilts. They are well rested despite having worked late. The restaurant must also have stayed open late, as witness its disorderly clutter of tables and chairs, the cigarette butts, fruit rinds and peels and shells of dried melon seeds strewn about on the floor and the unfinished food littering the tables. Whatever the exact closing time, it must be very late: why else has the mess been left until the morning to be cleaned up? Obviously it stayed open until everyone collapsed with fatigue. A girl working in the restaurant carelessly dumps the water in which mops and cleaning rags have been rinsed directly in the street outside the front door, and whoever catches the dirty waste water has only himself to blame for daring to walk into the path of the spill. Before the victim has time to protest, the employee would have turned and reentered the restaurant in all serenity.

The noontime peak starts about 11:30 a.m. and lasts until about 2 p.m. before business slackens off. By then not only the Little Restaurant but the entire alley quiets down and there is general weariness. The hair salons would be almost deserted and the hands of the girl washing a client's hair seem to doze off in the suds. The kids who have been playing in the alley have gone home to their pups and moms for a nap. Empty taxis cruise quietly through the alley. Under the bright sunshine, some peace and quiet, and cleanliness, reigns at this moment in the alley. Even the flies have been grounded. When people pass by, their footfall makes a crisp sound on the concrete pavement. The owner of the Little

Restaurant sits dozing in his usual place at the square table by the door, his deformed hand tucked in his lap, his legs crossed and his back hunched. Although he's known to only have a deformed hand, people somehow get the impression that he also suffers from some kind of leg disability: He almost never leaves this square table, not just because, it seems, he is guarding his cash box. He sits there contemplating the space in front and the passers-by. At mealtimes, an employee of his will spread cold plates, hot entrees and some rice wine on the square table for him to enjoy. He will savor the wine alone and take his time with his meal, interrupted only when he receives cash and dispenses change or has to help fill individual orders for box lunches. When he wakes up from his nap, the sun will have set some more and the light in the restaurant will be less glaring. He will then yawn and perk up a bit, his deformed hand uncurled and his elbows resting on the table edge, looking quite normal. The muted light or the nap has lifted the gloom on his face somewhat and his eyes are now livelier. Normally his eyes lack luster; you'd have a hard time categorizing them as either big or small, or as having double or single eyelids. Even in this late afternoon light, his eyes are amorphous, like Mongolian eyes. But now you can see that they have lighted up a bit and are moving alertly.

If you happen to pass by the Little Restaurant at this hour, you'll likely witness a scene of grotesque levity: girl employees washing his face and his feet. This is the liveliest moment of the day for the restaurant owner. He will laugh a child-like laugh, abandoning his face, his hands and feet to the girls—normally a minimum of two. He would banter and josh with them, his one mouth to their two mouths and two pairs of hands, as his face takes on an increasingly congenial look, his eyes and eyebrows no longer tightly knotted. You'd then become aware that his face has an oblong shape. This look on his face is more appropriate to the morning; it gives the impression that the day has only just started for the Little Restaurant. Don't be fooled into thinking he is single simply because he is often seen sitting alone and has girls washing his face and feet. Reality is otherwise. Let's go back to the story.

After the owner's hands and feet get washed, people start arriving. These are not patrons but friends. The girls put two rectangular tables side by side to form a square card table. The new arrivals sit around the table and start playing poker. The owner sits in his usual chair greeting and exchanging words with the guests in a high-pitched voice from a distance. Now completely awakened and perked up, he directs the girls to serve beverages. These arrivals are all local city folks who are the owner's buddies. They are the "smarter guys" in the saying: "Smarter girls marry wealthy bosses; smarter guys never have to work." They speculate on the stock market for a living and have a side job to which they pay only desultory attention. They appear to be thriving, without having to exert themselves too much. How else could they find spare time in the afternoon for a game of cards in the Little Restaurant? They most probably play with two decks of cards, because they number from 5 to 7 and one deck is definitely not enough. They drink tea or smoke their cigarettes as they play their cards with great seriousness. There is no boisterousness but a curious, unaccountable quiet tension in the air, even with so many players in the game. They are careful in playing their cards and meticulous in keeping score; they rarely exchange words unless they have something to say about the game itself. Yet somehow their eyes seem to tell you they are a little absent-minded and not totally focused on the game. There appears to be a second pair of eyes behind those glued to the cards.

These guests, like their host, have faces made amorphous by shadows on their forehead, eyelids, the hollows of their nose and the chin, blurring their outlines. Even without approaching them, you could smell the overnight halitosis from their mouth. The hands holding the cards are sticky and have the stale smell of fried peanuts. They deftly shuffle, deal out and play the cards, quickly finishing a game and immediately starting another. Card games should be a leisurely affair but not for them. Winning and scoring doesn't seem to be what motivates them to play quick successive games. Something else, like, for example, inertia, is driving them. They simply can't slow down; instead, the tempo quickens and excitement fills the air, accumulates and spreads. There is increasing anxiety.

In their distracted eyes, you suddenly become aware of a focused beam. You notice it in that fair-skinned young man wearing spectacles; or that half bald guy whose pea-like eyes are placed wide apart on either side of his flat nose. As you get to look at them more often, you gradually realize that beneath the shadows you invariably find on their faces they each possess some distinguishing marks by which you can tell them apart. Where are they projecting the focused beam of their sight? If you follow their line of sight past the card table, you discover that their eyes all converge on something by the window facing the alley. Under the barred window reclines a young woman in a rattan armchair, holding a cat in her lap. This is the owner's wife.

She looks very young, her round, delicate shoulders peeking out from under the fine lace trimming the collar of her silk sleeping gown. The loose-fitting sleeves of the gown, also trimmed with lace, have slipped down to her elbows, revealing a pair of white, plump forearms. A pair of strong but slender calves sticks out from under the laced hem of the gown. She wears a pair of red-strapped wooden clogs on her feet, the nails of whose round toes are colored with nail polish. Her fingernails are also painted with brightly-colored polish. Her hands, like her feet, smooth, plump and clean, are half buried in the plush, soft fur of the big, fat, white cat. Gold earrings dangle from her earlobes; a gold ring and a gold bracelet bedeck her hands while on her neck she wears a gold necklace. Curiously, so much gold has not made her look tacky and cheap, both because of the novel designs of the jewelry and the delicacy of her person. She has fine, good-looking facial features, and her heavy makeup has not obscured her healthy natural color and delicate skin. Hers is a strange dress style: pajamas combined with a heavy makeup more appropriate for a dinner party, and in the afternoon too. But that's the custom in this alley: You see similarly dressed sleeping beauties everywhere. Of course the lady owner of the Little Restaurant stands out in that she is more beautiful, more delicate and better cared for. She has never been seen with a broom or a cleaning rag, or children. All she does is recline in the rattan chair with her big, white cat, which has been spayed and now lazes about, without a shred of ambition. The mere sight of a cat nestled against a human in such sweltering weather is enough to make one sweat, yet neither she nor the cat seems to mind.

With her seated facing the alley all eyes are focused on a spot behind her ears. It is a particularly attractive spot: strands of hair cascading down, with the setting sun highlighting her nape and gilding the loose strands of hair into golden velvet. Those pairs of eyes have become piercing and undisguised, revealing some hidden suggestion. You sense that the lady owner is not unaware of these staring eyes, although she never once turns her head. And the owner sits unperturbed near the door, his eyes gazing into the deserted space in front of the restaurant, a smile hovering on his face. You realize that even he is not unaware of what's going on. And the girls, with nothing better to do in the lull than watching the card games, are privy to it. They may have left their native villages only recently, but they seem to have seen enough of the world to know. Everything in their faces tells you they are blasé about it, that they have each seen and done things themselves. Their skin has become fairer and their fingernails are properly trimmed under their meticulous care but more needs to be done before they can approach the perfection of their lady owner.

At this time even the chef has come out of the kitchen to watch the card games. He is a young man with clean, handsome features, with a white-complexion and sporting a winsome smile. He appears to be no older than 18, but is in fact definitely older than that. He would have to be at least 18, having graduated from a vocational high school, without counting the time already spent in the job market. But he must have only recently become a regular chef; otherwise long exposure to the grease and fumes in the kitchen would have browned him. He wears a clean, white smock and dons a white hat, which he has been carefully creased and sits smartly on his head. Everybody calls him

Didi ("younger brother"). He watches the games diffidently, without making a sound but paying close attention. He is the only one who truly follows the games. You'd never have guessed that a frail person like him could be equal to the task of preparing such a prodigious amount of food for boxed lunches plus the à la carte orders. Unlike others, he doesn't work late. As soon as he finishes his job for the evening, he goes home. If he is asked to stay late, he gets paid overtime. When it's time to punch out, about 9 p.m., he will take off his chef's white smock, change into his street clothes—a pair of leg-hugging black jeans, a black T-shirt and dark glasses, which he insists on wearing even when it is already dark. With the removal of his chef's hat, his hair is exposed. It's the new hedgehog unisex style sprayed with mousse. Protected by his hat, the hairdo has retained its shape and is free of the odor of kitchen fumes. On his feet he wears a pair of black shoes with a sharp toe and square heels. He walks out of the restaurant with a bright red helmet in his hand and hauls out his motorbike from the lumber yard across the road, where he parks his bike. He mounts his machine, straightens his back and starts the engine, which makes a deafening, self-righteous racket, and zooms away. People with his kind of skill never have to worry about finding a job anywhere they go. He leaves behind this little restaurant, with its muted lights and muffled voices, prostrate in the dark of the night.

The Story of Ah Qiao

1

He was known as Ah Qiao ("the knock-kneed one") for so long that few remembered his real name.

He had been born normal, all ruddy and wrinkled, like any newborn baby. His limbs were all there, albeit a tad on the small side. Nothing was missing: Where a pair was called for, he had a pair; where five were called for, he had all five. And he cried lustily enough.

Then he suffered a bout of polio. He

survived the days of high fever but the illness left him with a pair of spindly knock-knees. Although he was able to walk without a cane, he swayed with such exaggeration that the sight of him at once provoked laughter and was a strain on the eyes. Having adapted to the handicap, he walked at a fast pace and with practiced ease. He could even run, and as he did so, his fingertips could easily touch the inside of his forearms when he flailed his arms, much like a duck kicking its legs in water. This was another legacy of his childhood brush with polio.

His parents, hounded by a sense of guilt and remorse, were very indulgent toward him. At a very young age, when he and his younger brother had a hand in breaking of a pile of china plates, his brother was ordered to kneel on a washboard behind the door as punishment, while he got off lightly with a *maolizi* (literally "chestnut burr"), or a rap on the head with the first knuckle of the index or middle finger and sent out to play. When he got in trouble with neighborhood kids, his parents would always take his side, without first establishing where the fault lay, and say, "He is *qiaojiao* ("knock-kneed"). What could he have possibly done to you? Could he have beaten you or kicked you? He can't even keep his balance on his feet." The expression *qiaojiao* was a term of endearment used by his parents. It became so familiar to him since a tender age that he took it for granted and found it endearing, believing it to be his real name.

The neighbors sympathized with his plight and were initially quite forgiving and accommodating toward him. But there was only so much abuse they would take. People began grumbling. After all, the deformation of his legs was not the fault of the neighbors. People with leg deformations did not have a monopoly on misfortune. Those with healthy limbs might have other afflictions; they should not be expected to always humor him, defer to his whims or ask for his forgiveness. By and by people began treating him like an equal and would, when pushed to the wall, say, "*Qiaojiao*, you watch out. You'll get your comeuppance!" Although he was used to the appellation, he could sense the nuance in the tone and would turn bellicose with a curse: "F—— your mother!" or spit. The offender would then dodge and say, laughing, "Isn't that your name? Aren't you called Ah Qiao? Don't your mom and dad call you that?" Unable to contradict them, he would stalk away in a huff. After a few hours he would come up to the kid with a broad smile and a gift of candy, as if nothing had happened. He would call out helpfully, "Auntie, the rice is done. Let me take off the lid for you." While he received thanks, a smirk appeared on his face, because under the wrapper he had replaced the candy with a piece of soap and in the rice pot he'd sprinkled a pinch of coarse salt. As he imagined the auntie stamping her feet in frustration and the kid crying in disappointment, his heart swelled with satisfaction and happiness, so much so that he was put in a more generous mood and no longer minded so much what people called him. But his vicious antics got worse and started even to get on his parents' nerves. His long established prerogatives in the home, however, remained intact. At mealtime, he was the only one who assumed the right to grab a prized meat dish and eat directly from the bowl as if it were his personal portion, refusing to release the bowl despite the parental chopsticks knocking on his head. When it was time for the family members to cool themselves in the evening air, he was always the first to take possession of the rattan armchair, beating out the others, and wouldn't vacate it until the father rapped him with a cattail-leaf fan as he would swat a mosquito.

2

He started elementary school when the Cultural Revolution was launched. His parents naturally had excellent credentials to participate in this "Revolution," not only because they were workers but also because Ah Qiao's grandparents were destitute fishermen who had fled the impoverished north of Jiangsu Province to settle in the city. They had started out living in a crude, low shed patched together with straw mats in the Zhabei area of Shanghai and later moved into a thatch-roofed two-room dwelling they built, which was home for seven to eight people. The kids grew up crawling on the cold and damp clay floor. Who could be more revolutionary than they were? During the "Revolution," Ah Qiao's father made the acquaintance of someone who worked in the Housing Administration and they became comrades-in-arms. In an armed clash between factions the father covered the retreat of this comrade and was afterwards invited by the latter to dinner as a token of gratitude. The father accepted the invitation only upon the insistence of the comrade. The dinner was hosted in a first-rate fancy restaurant. It was a sumptuous feast, with dishes and drinks whose names he had never even heard of. So many courses were served that he lost count. The dinnerware was so bright and shiny, it dazzled his eyes. The long evening felt like a dream. After this feast, the father was haunted by an uneasy sense of indebtedness. To his mind, what he did for the comrade in the armed clash was unworthy of this honor. He wanted to reciprocate, but was worried that his modest circumstances would not allow him to honor the guest adequately. The mother thought otherwise, "True, our home is humble enough. He will feel cramped at the table but the food we serve will more than make up for the physical discomfort. Besides, it's the thought that counts." That helped make up the father's mind to invite the comrade to their home.

When the night of the dinner arriving, as the guest partook of the dishes, which were heavy on soy sauce—typical of the cuisine of north Jiangsu, such as *shizitou* ("lion's heads," or giant braised meatballs) and *hongshao tipang* (braised upper portion of a hog's leg), he looked around the damp, dark room and was moved to pity. He promised the father he'd find a decent apartment for them and, suiting action to word, he delivered a set of keys on the third night.

It came to pass that the year Ah Qiao started attending elementary school, his family moved into a south-facing big room on the ground floor of a double-width building in an old alley of Middle Huaihai Road, the most central, the busiest and the most "Shanghai-flavored" section of the city. The room had a second door that led to a little garden with an iron gate tightly secured by thick galvanized wire. One day, when his parents and siblings were busy mopping the floor and unpacking, Ah Qiao devoted full attention to the thick galvanized wire, which greatly fascinated him. Unable to get his hands on any tool and finding only a broken piece of brick, he used it to pound on the wire, and, after much pulling with his bloodied hands and

biting with his teeth, he finally pried the
wire loose. Then he had to deal with the
latch, which had rusted and fused with the
gate. After much expenditure of energy and
getting a dusting of rust on his hands and
all over his body, he was able to unlatch and
push open the gate. The heavy iron gate
swung open, with a groan, to reveal a wide,
tidy alley, across which could be seen the
back doors of the next row of apartments.
A little disappointed, his fun spoiled, he
pulled the gate in and was on the point of
withdrawing into his yard, when he spotted
a kid squatting on his heels outside a door
across the alleyway off to one side. The
kid was plump and had a fair-complexion,
fresh and tender, as if kneaded from dough.
Ah Qiao smiled as he was seized by an urge
to touch the kid. But the moment he took
a couple of steps in his direction, the kid
rose to his feet with a startled cry and ran
inside, slamming the door shut. Ah Qiao
froze in gaping incomprehension, clueless
as to what had happened. The warm feeling

inside him receded and vanished.

It was with some trepidation that he started going to school. As he saw those neatly dressed school kids, he developed a strong sense that he did not belong there. He was reluctant to open his mouth to speak for fear of betraying his north Jiangsu accent. Where they'd come from, the north Jiangsu dialect was the first language and kids who didn't speak it had to learn to speak that dialect in order to be accepted. But here everyone spoke the ear-soothing Shanghainese dialect. He felt so different from the others and so alone. After school he always rushed home with his book bag and the mandatory bag containing the book of Chairman Mao's quotations. But he felt no less alone at home. All the doors in the neighborhood were tightly shut and few kids were seen to play outside. He would occasionally see a couple of kids playing some distance away, but they played among themselves, speaking in lowered tones and would scatter and disappear the moment

their parents called out to them. His dejection
was short-lived. His spirits were lifted one
day by a group of Red Guards moving into
the neighborhood, pounding savagely on
doors. When the door was opened, the Red
Guards would storm into the apartment.
When he tried to follow them in, he was
barred by red guards stationed at the door.
He explained to them, "I belong to the Five-
red Categories (politically favored classes
of poor peasants, lower-middle peasants,
soldiers, cadres and the dependents of
revolutionary martyrs)." Nobody gave
him any attention, so he was reduced,
leaning against the wall outside. The sharp
rebukes and the sound of breaking glass
in the interior of the apartment tantalized
him. Then an idea hit him. Leaping up, he
grabbed an overhanging oleander branch
and, his legs flailing against the wall, he
heaved himself up the low fence wall; but
the colored glass shards set into the top of
the wall cut his hands. "F——!" he cursed.
He broke off a twig and started whipping

the glass shards with it, sending the colored slivers of glass in all directions, until all the glass shards were gone from the top of the wall. Throwing away the branch he let out a long breath of satisfaction. He sat on the fence wall, observing the chaos going on inside the apartment with an immense sense of happiness.

From that moment on, he no longer felt a need to tiptoe around others or to live in perpetual trepidation. Besides, he was speaking Shanghainese now with greater fluency and began to gradually blend in at school and in the neighborhood. He would watch others play from the sidelines, staying close to remind people of his presence. He would show off games only he knew how to play to attract the attention of other kids. In his thirst for companionship, he tried unrealistically to take advantage of every opportunity to mingle and win acceptance. He did all he could to catch crickets to offer to his school mates. He recounted crude jokes brought home by his parents from their workplaces to classmates in a bid to win their affection. Once he even consented to a game of tag. Every time he started running, the others would double up in laughter; even the passers-by would pause to look. The laughter continued even when he stopped running; when he resumed running, people would laugh with a vengeance, so much so some rolled on the ground with mirth. He no longer knew what to do; despite feeling embarrassed and hurt, he took it on the chin, even laughing with the others, who never noticed the tears in his eyes amid the general laughter.

In a military training class, a mischievous classmate raised his hand to volunteer Ah Qiao for a short race planned for that day, causing uproarious laughter in the class. The teacher couldn't help laughing himself after angrily reprimanding the wag. Since the culprit had been duly disciplined, there was nothing Ah Qiao could do but laugh with everyone else. This caused some to whisper among themselves, "He is really thick-skinned." The military training class was followed by a political indoctrination class held indoors. Back in the classroom the prankster, who was going to sharpen his pencil in his sharpener, found a segment of an earthworm stuffed in it. Startled, he threw it away but then decided to pursue the matter further. He retrieved the sharpener with a trembling hand and handed it to the teacher, who turned out to be even more scared of squirmy worms and threw it away even farther—this time outside the window. There was no way the pencil sharpener could ever be found again once it landed in the heavily trafficked street outside. The teacher put it down to another prank pulled by that student, who tied himself in knots trying to explain but finally gave up and cried.

After school that day Ah Qiao headed home in a buoyant mood, kicking a stone along. Suddenly he was surprised by a shrill cry ahead of him. Looking up from the stone he was kicking, he saw a pair of plump little legs, fair as white lotus root, scissoring furiously in a headlong dash. When he instinctively gave chase, the plump legs quickened their scissoring motions until the plump boy tripped, fell down and started bawling. An adult came out of a door, picked up the owner of the plump legs, comforting him and taking Ah Qiao to task, "You scared the kid! What if he becomes ill from the fright?"

He was suddenly made aware of the power he wielded and made successful use of it on many subsequent occasions to menace others.

3

In the meantime his obstreperousness was increasingly taxing the patience of his parents, who now transferred their pity-induced affection for him to his healthy siblings. While he was not observed to behave in a suspicious way, strange things were happening frequently in the home: the mini-edition of *Chairman Mao's Selected Works*, much cherished by his father, disappeared. After the whole house was turned upside down in the search for it, it turned up one day under a pillow, safe and sound. The mother's ox horn comb, whose teeth were already sparse enough, was unaccountably losing more teeth every day. His younger brothers never won a fight with him over food and always ended up crying. His parents would come after him to mete out some corporal punishment but he would run out like lightning into the alleyway. When the father stopped, he would stop too and turn about with a provocative smile, baring his neat, white teeth, causing his father to gnash his teeth and curse, "You bastard! You Ah Qiao (knock-knees)!"

The neighbors, who were by now on a more familiar basis with him, also started calling him Ah Qiao, taking a cue from his father. He remained unperturbed, raising no objections to the moniker. But one day, when the culverts in the alley clogged up, inundating the street with fetid water, the sewage workers sent from the Housing Administration dug out a large chunk of rags and rotten vegetable leaves. The neighbors immediately started accusing one another of carelessness and sloth. Amid the noisy recriminations, no one paid much attention to the boy squatting outside a door not too far away, quietly picking his nose. He slowly got to his feet and ambled through the crowd, momentarily silencing the neighbors, who watched him make his way toward the mouth of the alley. Someone said in a lowered voice, "Sneaky bastard!"

He didn't hear it and kept on going. Once out of the alley and into the street, he sat in a street garden, watching the busy traffic and the passers-by. When he saw a nice-looking girl, he picked up some stones and threw them at her, sometimes missing his target. When the projectile was on target, the girl cried with a start and turned about to look for the culprit. When her eyes fell on him, she found him bent over an ant, all absorbed in an attempt to drown it in his spit.

From sitting much of the time at the mouth of the alley, he got acquainted with the troublemakers of other nearby alleys. They became fast friends with him, making him their leader because they worshipped his outlandish, quirky ideas and tricks. These children were much younger; and only children of a tender age would worship someone like him, because they didn't know better. But if you stood them next to Ah Qiao, you wouldn't be able to tell the difference in age. Apparently he had stopped growing. Although he was already in secondary school, he looked like someone in his low teens, short and scrawny, sallow-faced, with reedy limbs. Those attuned to the facts knew, however, that those limbs, as puny and unsightly as they might look, served him well. Since acquiring a following, he no longer needed to exercise his legs much; he would sit there sticking the little ones on pretty girls and any youngster who looked like a good student, or a mental patient on Huaihai Road, on whom they ragged shamelessly. He personally waded into battle only at the crucial or climactic moment. The minute he kicked up his legs, they would splay out at incredible angles from the knees down and swing in such a wide circle that nobody could come within two meters of him. His hands reaching the inside of his forearms added to his bluster. As the rivals dispersed in disarray, his followers would clap and cheer. In order to enjoy this joyous, exciting scenario more often, his followers would sometimes exaggerate the danger of defeat to goad him into joining the fray. Although well aware of the trick, he went along willingly because it brought him great satisfaction.

As the little kids grew up, their height exceeded his by a head or half a head and they acquired a stocky build. Physically they appeared to be his senior but his face gave his age away: You couldn't find any wrinkles on the sallow face but somehow it had a shriveled, weathered look. The kids gradually saw through him and no longer found his company desirable. They deserted him, finding better things to do. Sometimes they would walk right past him on the street as if they were total strangers. He would curse under his breath, "F—— your mother!" and, still unappeased, would throw a handful of sand after the offending party.

4

When he finished middle school, he still looked like a 10-year-old boy. There was nothing to be done about it.

Although the *yipianhong* policy (literally "red all across the country," a policy of sending middle school students to the countryside across China during the Cultural Revolution) no longer hung like a sword of Damocles over the middle school

graduates that year, rumors were rife. Amid
general anxiety among the students, he
alone was unperturbed. No matter how
wide the "red" tide spread, he was sure to be
allowed to stay in Shanghai, even if the king
of heaven got sent away to the backwaters.
He was destined to stay in Shanghai and be
a Shanghai resident till the end of time. The
confusion and unease around him gave him
great satisfaction.

He was assigned to a neighborhood
production group, where he worked winding
electric coils. But his pair of hands soon
proved unequal to this kind of delicate work
and he was shifted to materials distribution
and handling and storage of finished coils.
This was less boring than sitting at a bench
winding coils for eight hours a day. Shuttling
between the workbenches in the factory, he
got to know a lot of people, mostly girls,
some of whom were far from bad-looking.
They all called him Ah Qiao. He didn't find
it offensive, coming from the girls; he rather
liked this nickname being pronounced

by the girls in a coquettish or even in a truculent way. Probably his puny physique and his disability disarmed the girls, who were quite affectionate toward him. In contrast, their attitude toward the male electric workers in the factory was at best reserved and icy, pokerfaced, discouraging any attempt at conversation. With him, the girls were relaxed and familiar, constantly sparring playfully, sometimes hitting him on the shoulder, or the back or even the top of the head when the sparring got them excited. And he enjoyed that kind of familiarity.

Once he started gainful employment, his status in the home improved. After drawing his first salary, he received a navy blue casual shirt made of Dacron as a gift form his mother. When he walked into the street wearing the new shirt, he received compliments.

"Ah Qiao, you are fashionable now! You look impressive!"

He smiled coyly, saying nothing.

Ah Qiao was not without a heart. If you treated him nicely, he would treat you nicely too. He was a dutiful son. When he bought a slice of pork jowl for thirty cents to go with his father's wine, his father surprised him by pouring him half a glass. The father became much more congenial when he had someone to drink with.

This was the happiest period in Ah Qiao's life. But happiness often proves ephemeral.

5

The Gang of Four was overthrown. After the parades, the fireworks, the celebrations and euphoria, there were things that needed to be dealt with.

The first thing he and his family needed to tackle concerned the apartment. It was the private property of the owner of a silks and fabrics store, who raised the matter of repossession daily with the Housing Administration. The Housing

Administration in turn raised the matter
with them, every three or five days, if
not daily. His father sought help from his
old friend and comrade-in-arms in the
Administration, but the friend had been
disgraced and sidelined and was busy day
and night preparing his "detailed account"
of his behavior in the recent past. Faced
with his own precarious plight, he was in no
condition to think about others' troubles.
The consensus reached in the family
was that their eviction was a foregone
conclusion, dictated by the circumstances,
as was their move into the apartment. But
maybe they wouldn't necessarily be forcibly
expelled, since they were already living in
the apartment. They decided to ask for quid
pro quos from the Housing Administration.
They'd move out if their demands were
met; if not, then nobody could blame
them for not vacating the apartment. Once
the decision was made, they felt better,
but a bitterness rankled in their hearts.
Production was halted and people lost their

lives in the Cultural Revolution; after so many years of tumult, there was a sudden reversal and everything returned to the status quo ante. It appeared the revolution had been much ado about nothing after all. Come to think of it, it was always the poor who suffered most, which led the mother to cite the popular saying: "If 9.9 liters of grain is your lot, you'll never get a decaliter like it or not."

When presented with their proposal, the Housing Administration went wide-eyed before agreeing to study it. The study was followed by a counteroffer by the administration, and a counter counteroffer, which was taken back for further study. A few days later new demands were raised by the family after consultation among its members. There were more wide-eyed shocks, more studies and more bargaining… in the endless haggling, they got to stay one more year in the apartment, a year in which their only preoccupation was negotiations, and life became an afterthought.

It was at this time that the students previously sent to the countryside were starting to return to the cities. The young men and women who were swarthy and sallow-faced only the day before now wore high heels and rode fast, brand new Phoenix bicycles to work. Ah Qiao's superiority evaporated before he knew it and the Dacron shirt was no longer in vogue, overtaken now by the more popular zippered shirts, youth shirts and Shanghai shirts. The Dacron shirt was so sturdy it didn't look as if it was going to unravel anytime soon, so there was no excuse to buy a new one.

Curiously he no longer found solace in the familiar joshing of the girls in the factory. As the electric workers quietly found their regular dates and went out to lunch together or to see the movies, he began to feel something was missing in his life. When their girlfriends made uncensored jokes at his expense, the male workers found nothing wrong with it and laughed along, without showing the least trace of jealousy. This embittered him and stoked a nameless anger. He began to resent the flirting of the girls and put on a stern face to discourage their familiarity. But they were not about to let him off so lightly and teased him in various ways, "Ah Qiao, why do you look so sad?" "Ah Qiao, you look so serious! Are you being inducted into the Communist Youth League?" "Ah Qiao, you must want a girlfriend badly. Should I find you one?" They were not older than him; as a matter of fact some were much younger but everyone treated him as a child who had stopped growing. In their pursuit of fun at his expense, they forgot that he too had emotions and desires and that he wanted to have a girlfriend like everyone else. Once when pushed to a corner by a teasing girl, he answered:

"I don't want you to find a girl for me. I want you."

There was general laughter, "Ah Qiao is really funny."

Even the girl's boyfriend laughed with

the rest. "I'll cede her to you. No problem. I'm generous and selfless."

Someone gave Ah Qiao a shove toward the girl, causing her to shriek.

Putting on a stern face proved ineffective. It only struck people as odd and put extra strain on him. Why not relax and be laid-back! He knew how to take it as it comes. Otherwise he would have been miserable all these past years. Because of his ability to take things in stride, life had not been so miserable but rather punctuated by fun moments.

Thus rationalizing, he decided to go with the convivial mood of the others. Coming out of the passive mode and going on the offensive proved rewarding. When the girls slapped him on his back or some other parts, he would slap back, gently, and a fond, heartwarming memory was born in the middle of his palm. When the girls went too far, the girl sitting by the south window at the far end of the table would intervene in a soft voice, "Quit bothering him! Stop

it! Poor Ah Qiao." Although her voice was
drowned out by the ambient noise, he heard
it distinctly and took a good look at her.
As he looked at her some more, a curious
quivering arose in his heart. The girl was not
good-looking but had a fair-complexion.
Never one to care about his own looks and
grooming, he had a special weakness for
white complexions. So he started taking
special care of her. One day, a coil was
sloppily wound by her, he surreptitiously
switched it with one in the next worker's
bin and yelled, "Who did this one? It's a
sloppy piece of work." And he held it up for
everyone to see. The girl sitting next to the
maker of that bungled coil cried foul, "It's
not my work." "It's not yours? Then whose
is it?" As he said this, he sneaked a look at
the girl he was protecting, who continued
to work serenely, her head bowed and her
eyes lowered, totally unaware of his effort
to cover her imperfection. Feeling deflated,
he dropped his arm. He found her lunch
skimpy, with the box half filled with rice,

upon which were sparsely spread a little bit of vegetable and a few pieces of sausage. Moved to pity, he took out a brined egg from his pant pocket one day when no one else was around at lunch time, and sent it rolling toward her, saying, "It's for you." He was unprepared for her reaction: She cringed with fright, pushing her back tightly against the back of her chair, dodging the egg, which rolled past her and fell to the floor, breaking to pieces. Her fright almost gave the impression that a bomb had been lobbed against her. The look of disgust in her face reminded one of the revulsion at the sight of a dirty rat.

With the breaking of the egg, he felt a pang in his heart, as if some part of it had broken along with the ill-fated egg. But the sense of heartbreak disappeared along with the dying of the sound of breakage, leaving him very bitter. "This is no way to repay a kindness." Uncharacteristically he didn't use the word "F——!"

Of late he had discovered an unusual

aftertaste associated with the obscenities he'd used freely since childhood. He couldn't get over the fact that he had used the obscenity for so many years without getting its meaning. He understood even less how he could have used curses he didn't understand for so many years. The new revelation caused him to tremble with excitement. So that's what it means, he thought. The new discovery disturbed his peace and made him irascible. Simply because his father said, "When you chew your food, you sound like a pig," he flung his bowl on the floor and ran out of the house. As he walked on the busy Huaihai Road, he felt extremely lonely. Suddenly all the passers-by around him looked happier than he was. Some looked over their shoulder at him after passing him, astonishment in their eyes; others, equally astounded, walked by impassively without showing any emotion. He cursed, "F—— your mother!" As he did so, he felt an involuntary thrill.

Every night, exercising his fertile imagination and using the familiar obscenities as dictionary, he wove some lurid story to soothe his unsettled, troubled soul till the wee hours. During the daytime hours, there were too many things going on for him to make up his story undistracted. Involuntarily drawn into the bantering and laughter around him, he went wild with x-rated language of his own concoction, frightening his company.

6

The girls in the workshop got married one after another. Every time he had to chip in to buy a gift: fifty cents, a dollar, two dollars, and growing as the consumer price index inched up. And of course he'd get his share of the "wedding sweets": two packs of candies, eight to a pack. The candies had a curious taste in his mouth. As he chewed them slowly, an inexplicable sadness suffused his being.

Not long after the taste of the wedding sweets faded in his mouth, the girls' bellies became increasingly prominent, bursting open the buttoned slit of their pants to reveal immodestly the hitherto mysterious pattern on the underwear, the sight of which made his head swim. Oblivious to all this, they continued their exchanges about what went on inside there. Sometimes they would huddle and keep their conspiratorial voices down as far as possible in a seemingly speechless discussion. He couldn't figure out what they were up to, try as he might. To his mind their uncommon, prominent bellies were nothing less than awe-inspiring.

As a consequence, they shifted much of their attention away from Ah Qiao, which meant he had more quiet moments to himself and more time to think about things. Sometimes he thought about himself and found out there was not much to think about in that department. One bustling day after another, he went from workbench to workbench, making fun of people and being made fun of. His hands and his mouth never knew a moment of rest. After so many years on the job, he still didn't know what kind of parts or components he was handling, or whether they were to be installed in a radio or a television. The volumes of words issuing out of his mouth were unintelligible even to himself, lost like a thin stream in desert sand. Back when he was in school, he had read some books that he never managed to understand, or sat where the alley ended in the street, watching the traffic, both vehicular and human. He didn't know why he was required to read those books or where the cars and pedestrians came from or were heading to. As his mind ventured further back in time, things became a little blurry. Under the eaves of the crowded shanties, he would urinate at the wall to flush out crickets. The base of the wall eventually was softened by the urine. Going back further the only thing he could remember was the sound of angry or joyous cries of "Ah Qiao! Ah Qiao!" He got bored by all those memories and a sadness would came over him. He became very quiet.

When someone remembered his presence and quipped, "Ah Qiao, when are we going to get wedding sweets from you?" he would swear, dour-faced, "F—— your mother!" Now the tone was very different, seriously venomous and threatening, so people knew better than to ruffle his feathers and left him alone in his self-imposed state of non-communication.

When he wanted to break out of his glum silence to unwind himself for a bit, he would say to a girl with a recently prominent belly, "From your physiognomy, I can tell you'll not give birth to a male heir." The female worker shot back angrily, "I don't care if I get a male heir, as long as my baby is not born with knock-knees." Stung to the quick and chastened, he couldn't even bring himself to utter his usual profanity "F——!" because he knew he had it coming. He bungled the jokes. His jokes had become rusty. Sometimes the joke would have a promising start; there would be good-natured bantering. The girl might slap him playfully and he repaid in kind, unfortunately with a little more force than he'd intended. She would scream and rain blows on his back, no longer in jest now. Feeling the pain inflicted by her fists, he hit back, stunning the girl, who stared at him in disbelief. His face distorted by anger frightened her, deterring her from continuing the fisticuffs. The only thing left for her to do was cry at the top of her lungs and curse, "Ah Qiao! Ah Qiao! Why don't you drop dead!" He had a shiver of realization. He seemed to have only now realized the meaning of this familiar nickname that had accompanied him since a child.

From the moment of realization on he became sulky, nursing a grudge against everybody, whether justified or not. He no longer bantered with those around him and became generally very taciturn. His rare verbal outbursts were often frightening, so people tiptoed around him and discussed him in whispers.

"What happened to Ah Qiao? He has become so menacing."

"I don't know. Scary!"

"Ah Qiao is not young anymore. Must be over 20."

"Over 25 is more like it."

He walked past them with a glum face, pretending not to have overheard them but mentally trying to figure out his age. Few ever thought about how old he was, a subject to which he never gave much serious thought either. Days, months and years just grinded on. He walked on with the raw materials in his arms and the question of his age on his mind. Nowadays he took pains to take shorter steps when he walked to keep his balance and maintain a better poise. But it proved difficult and only made walking more tiring. He had never before found walking to be an onerous task but now he did. He went to see the group leader and asked to be assigned to other tasks that did not require so much walking. The group leader was in a quandary. She couldn't think of anything else he was capable of doing but on the other hand she was leery of upsetting him. Somehow she felt that if she riled him, she would be hit with disastrous consequences. Luckily for her the dilemma was solved without her intervention, through an unexpected external event. Orders came down from on high that all middle school students who graduated during the "Great Cultural Revolution" were to take a national examination to recertify their diplomas. The workplaces were to provide free time for those workers concerned to brush up on their studies and those who failed the exam would see their bonuses cut. She decided to give Ah Qiao one month of study leave to prepare for the first such examination.

7

He started boning up at home. Even his parents felt it was unfair to him: "It's not your fault that you didn't perform well in school. The Gang of Four is solely to blame." He would retort, "What's the point of saying this to me?" He said this not because he willingly supported the idea of the national recertification exam. In fact he resented it very much at heart and had uttered, aloud or under his breath, "F——!" a hundred times. But he was also tired of his parents' nagging and fussing, having at some point of time included his parents in his hate list. He believed that his parents had control over and were responsible for his knock-knees, seeing that his siblings were all healthy and fully equipped. He therefore seemed to reserve an extra intensity of hate for the parents.

At his retort, his parents said with a sneer, "So you will pass the exam. You are an academic type."

In anger he flung the table over.

For the first few days he sat in an auto shop in the next alley, listening to the lectures of a tutor hired for four yuan a night. He kept yawning and craved sleep. Lowering

his eyes, he found the book practically
written in undecipherable divine code;
raising his eyes he found the blackboard
scribbled with what appeared like esoteric
Eight Trigrams. He fretted, thinking that
his bonus was as good as gone, but it never
amounted to much anyway, so who cared.
And that helped make up his mind against
taking the exam. No longer feeling bound
by the books and lectures, he perked up, the
yawns and sleepiness suddenly gone. There
was no point just sitting there twiddling
his thumbs, so he listened desultorily, and
gradually picked up fresh ideas here and
there. Ah Qiao was not born with a dense
mind. He had a sharp mind, except that he
rarely made good use of it. If he put his mind
to it, he would be able to handle the books.
Since there was nothing else to occupy him
at home, he began browsing through the
books, which turned out not to be so hard.
He thus developed a greater interest in
reading. And when it was time to take the
exam, he passed it with flying colors. When

he returned to work, the other workers in
his group looked at him with fresh eyes,
saying playfully:

"I never knew Ah Qiao had such
wonderful talents."

"Ah Qiao is so good with books. He has
bright promise."

"Ah Qiao is meant to be an intellectual."

He didn't say anything but only smiled,
the fierceness in his eyes softened somewhat.
Faced with such plaudits, he found it hard to
sulk and ask for a transfer. He continued to
transport materials between workbenches,
taking care to keep his movements well
modulated when he walked and trying his
best to keep his back straight to maintain
good posture. Walking thus became more
onerous for him.

It was a time when dance parties became
popular. New Year's Eve, National Day, May
First Labor Day, May Fourth Youth Day, all
kinds of award ceremonies, you name it,
were all perfectly good excuses for holding
dance parties. With some kind of dance floor

prepared, the boom box turned on, people would gather around an empty dance floor, giggling and pushing each other toward the center of the floor, as if it were not a dance floor but a pond. Those being shoved would struggle to keep their footing on the shore and those unlucky enough to land in the water would scurry back only to find a wall of bystanders blocking his return, so he would try to drag them into the pond with him.

Ah Qiao joined the fray and was intent on shoving others onto the floor, using such force that he often sent them tottering toward the dance floor. With tune after tune played, nobody went in and none left. Music excited him; he enjoyed listening to music, whether it had a throbbing beat or a leisurely rhythm. It was only when the party was drawing to a close that people mustered enough courage and began to step onto the dance floor, bashfully and with the utmost reluctance, their faces flushed, as if it were the partners who had dragged them in against their will. It began with one or two couples, then it grew to three or five. Eventually the dance floor filled up, overflowing with dancing couples in a setting that now resembled a small food mart with shoppers jostling each other. The difference was that here, if you jostled somebody or stepped on someone's toes, you didn't use abusive language as you would in a food mart but tried to be civil and deferential to each other as etiquette required.

Soon everybody started dancing. Besides social dancing, there was also disco which was performed with the two legs moving as if treading on a waterwheel. Ah Qiao left the dance quietly and unobtrusively, taking care not to bump against anyone or drawing attention. He felt very lonely.

At the height of the "dance parties" rage, people had a hard time keeping their behind on a chair. They were always talking about the three-steps, four-steps, the waltz or the rumba.

"I saw a couple dancing like this, see?" A girl demonstrated the steps to the girl on the opposite side of the workbench.

"Oh, that's knock-kneed rumba."

"Knock-kneed rumba?"

"Don't you know knock-kneed rumba?" The surprise was accompanied by scorn.

The other girl cautioned her by kicking her under the table. "Keep your voice down! Ah Qiao might hear you."

"It's not as if we are talking about him," she said this unconcernedly, but looked around just in case and found Ah Qiao standing right by her ready to collect her finished coils. She felt a little awkward and muttered, "Ah Qiao, we were not talking about you. Don't be cross."

"It would be fine even if you were talking about me," Ah Qiao said with some sincerity.

"Seriously, we meant no offense." His leniency only made her more flustered and she tried to explain, flush-faced.

Ah Qiao walked away, knock-kneed and

without a word. He felt a tightening of his chest and something seemed on the verge of overflowing his eyes but didn't.

8

There was another newfangled idea inspired from above, this time to hold a meeting to hear speeches centered on the subject of revitalization of the nation. Every factory was to recommend a speaker to the district leadership. When nobody volunteered, the leadership had to designate someone and Ah Qiao was picked. Everybody said, "Very good. It's a good choice. Ah Qiao can talk about the national recertification exam." "Those in favor of the choice, please raise your hand." And all hands shot up. "The choice has been adopted unanimously!" This left Ah Qiao furious, gnashing his teeth and mouthing the vilest obscenities but nobody heard him. The crowd dispersed. The group leader tried to cheer him. "Everybody voted for you. It's an honor, so just do it."

"Yes, it's an honor and I am doing it. You just wait and see."

"Don't come to work tomorrow. Stay home to prepare the speech."

"Yes, I need to be well-prepared."

"Don't be mad. People voted for you in good will." The group leader began to feel worried.

"I know they had my welfare at heart. I will give the speech. I'm all for national revitalization." With that, he turned and left, in long strides, the bottoms of his flared jeans sweeping the street surface.

The next day he didn't come to work, but he didn't prepare his speech either and slept through the day. He read a few news articles about someone who was murdered and whose body was cut up into pieces, and a crime in which the victim's head was missing. On the third day, the group leader asked, scanning his face with some concern, "Have you prepared the speech?"

"I have. I'm well-prepared." The way he said this with a smile sent a chill down the spine of the group leader.

"Are you really well-prepared?" she asked after a pause.

"Really. See you at the meeting."

Her misgivings deepened. "If you really don't want to do it, I can find someone else."

"Auntie, you must be kidding. Day before yesterday when I said I didn't want to do it, you insisted that I did it. Now that I'm prepared, you want to prevent me doing it."

"Who says I don't want you to do it? I'll be thrilled if you agree to make the speech," the group leader hastened to say before walking away.

On the day of the event, which was held in the auditorium of the district Culture House, all seats were taken. A purple velvet curtain hung over the podium, illuminated by bright lighting; on the apron of the stage sat a row of colorful flowers in full bloom.

Most of the workers were there and he sat next to the group leader, who was filled with unease. She said gently to him, "Relax! Speak slowly."

"I won't speak fast, Auntie. Don't worry," he replied.

Auntie was now regretting her decision to designate him as the speaker but it was too late and all she could do was cross her fingers and hope for the best.

The meeting was declared open and the speakers did their level best. They were neatly dressed and spoke Mandarin with perfect diction. Their facial expressions were lively. The more speakers she heard, the more troubled the group leader became. She turned to look at Ah Qiao and found him calm and self-assured. She wondered what kind of brilliant performance he had rehearsed for the event.

Finally it was his turn.

Getting up from his seat, he moved toward the podium, knock-kneed and nonchalant, in sweeping motions, his feet spaced a meter apart and his hands swinging in flowing wide arcs in sync with the swaying of his body.

The assembly fell silent, their eyes fixed on him.

He began to feel some unease and modulated his movements.

In the general hush, countless pairs of eyes were trained on him.

He strained to shrink his strides and slightly bent his head to watch his two deformed legs shamble soundlessly across the green grass turf carpet. The carpet seemed endless, stretching all the way to the foot of the stage, which he couldn't see. The carpet was laid on a floor with a slight incline and he was drawn forward by gravity and had some difficulty maintaining his balance. He began to regret having chosen to sit in the last row with a view to giving himself plenty of time to make a fool of himself and pulling a nasty prank on the assembly and his factory. But he hadn't expected it to be such a long walk.

And the quiet in the hall was getting on his nerves. Drops of sweat began to form on his forehead.

There was a general hush and countless pairs of eyes were staring at him.

His back was drenched in sweat and his shirt was soaking wet. Slowly he clasped his deformed hands together as he walked on. But the road was long and slightly inclined. He was walking down a gentle slope and he had to steady his feet to keep himself from stumbling.

There was an absolute silence in the hall.

He walked carefully, his mind cleared of anything other than the walk. He had to strain and think for every step he took. He crossed the green turf carpet step by soundless step, as if walking down a green, gently inclined trail. But how long the walk was! He felt the high vault over the auditorium weigh heavily on him.

He finally came to the foot of the podium and climbed the steps. Behind the drapes on stage many eyes were observing him in silence. He went on stage.

The dazzling, incandescent lighting enveloped him, making him feel suffocated.

He felt a shortness of breath. His breathing became labored.

All of a sudden the audience exploded into thunderous applause, making him wince, unsure what was happening.

The storm-like, thundering applause was long and drawn-out. It lasted and lasted.

He was stunned and froze on stage, not knowing why he was standing up there and what he was doing there.

The applause went on and on.

Dazzled by the bright light, he could see nothing, except that the all-enveloping brightness was expanding with solemnity. There seemed to be no limit to the expansion.

The applause went on.

He was melted by the dazzling, incandescent light. He didn't know if he still existed.

The applause died down and quiet

returned to the hall, so quiet you could hear people breathing. He had never experienced such an absolute quiet. He stood in place in a daze, then turned and walked back down the stage.

A lump rose in his throat, there was a pull at the corners of his mouth and something finally welled out of his eyes.

Something welled out of his eyes, down his cheeks slowly, into his mouth. It had a salty taste and he swallowed it.

The Nest Fight

After leaving the employ of the Xie family, Auntie Xiaomei found another job with a family in a nearby apartment building on Yuyuan Road. Actually the apartment was shared by two families, with her new employer occupying one large and one smaller room. The couple had the smaller room and Auntie Xiaomei shared the large room with two kids who were in grade school. The large room also doubled as living room and dining room. Although it was the larger of the two rooms, it scarcely had any room after being furnished with three single beds and a dining table. Consequently Auntie Xiaomei had no alternative but to leave some of her belongings in the temporary care of her former employer, including a rosewood chest of drawers, three camphor wood trunks, her household registration and her rations of cereals and cooking oil. She had no intention to stay long in her new job. She would leave as soon as she found a job more to her liking. Luckily for her, the lady of the Xie family was very accommodating and obliging in the matter of the temporary storage of her things.

Life in the new family was relatively simple and modest, depriving Auntie Xiaomei of an arena to deploy her finely honed housekeeping skills. The drive and aggressiveness she had when she was in her prime had been worn down by the vagaries of life. She no longer rushed headlong into the future but began to think more about a graceful old age. At night she lay in her bed in the room crammed with bare wood furniture, her ears assailed by the duet of the snoring of the two kids. The light from the moon and from the streetlamps penetrated the flimsy printed fabric of the window drapes to flood the room, making her feel uncovered, as though she were sleeping in the street. Unable to fall asleep, she passed the events in her life in review, rewinding the past and looking at it frame by frame: The day she entered the household of one of the most prominent families of Hangzhou as a maid servant, her hair tied behind her head into a pigtail with a two-inch red string and her silk blouse and silk pants trimmed at the hems and along the edges with lacework; the day she followed the eldest daughter of the family, as her personal maid, to Shanghai when the daughter was married into the Zhang family, where she had waited on the newlywed mistress until she became the venerable elderly lady of the house and eventually passed on. Upon her mistress's death, her employment was terminated by the next generation of the Zhang family and she moved on to the Xie family before coming here. Throughout these decades of service, she had witness the departure of the old, the birth of the young, the growth of the young into adulthood and their death. In the end she remained a family of one. She did save some money but she had found no good use for it, and the money had become something like a lonely neglected ghost. These thoughts deeply saddened her. A proud soul all her life, she had ended up working for others, living on sufferance and taking care not to displease her employers. With the passage of time, her physical strength had been declining steadily, a reality she had to come to terms with. If she should become too old and frail to continue this kind of work, she would have no place to go. She couldn't very well go back to her native village near Hangzhou. After all these years she had long become a Shanghainese, and she had never considered herself a country woman. She, Auntie Xiaomei, was Shanghainese! A Shanghainese had to live in Shanghai;

nothing could be more natural and logical. Yet, this was how she felt about Shanghai. How Shanghai felt about her was less clear and certain. This caused her to somewhat regret not having gotten married when she was younger. But when she was in her prime she had great expectations, an irrepressible energy, inexhaustible resourcefulness and her whole life in front of her … She would became drowsy and dozed off in this dejected state, but no sooner would she close her eyes than she would hear the swishing sound of a broom sweeping the pavement outside the building. It was time to get up and buy the day's groceries. She got up with an effort, her shoulders and back still sore and her eyelids heavy. She couldn't stop yawning. Another day's gloom was now added to the previous day's gloom, which had yet to dissipate. The accumulative gloom had caused Auntie Xiaomei to visibly wither.

After many nights of soul searching, Auntie Xiaomei finally came to the realization that she needed a place of her own. A home is a nest; a nest means a house. With a house she would have a place to stay. She would no longer need to be lodged in someone else's apartment. Instead of working full-time, she could offer her service in buying groceries, doing laundry or cooking meals—either lunch or dinner for others. Her total income would be more, not less, than what she was earning now. Besides, money was not a big concern of hers. If she so chose, she could stay home and live on her savings without having to work another day in her life. But first of all she needed a home. Naturally in the matter of money, the more one had the better. With a place of her own, she could think of many more ways of making money. She could buy a sewing machine and make dresses for people. She did not have the skills to make western-style dresses but she was familiar with Chinese dressmaking, including the techniques of teasing silk floss and relining silk floss quilted jackets. It would be work that was more leisurely in pace, cleaner and more respectable. She could also apply at the neighborhood office for a factory job. That would mean that her life, and illnesses and death, would be substantially provided for by the state. Then she could adopt a son. When she had a son, everything she had would have a repository and all the hard work she had done would have an enduring meaning. The thought of having a son to call her own greatly boosted her spirits but at the same time left her wistful. Anyway, she thought, once she had a house, many options would be opened up, and all paths would become passable; without a home, the only path before her would be a narrow one that would keep narrowing. This new realization rather calmed her down, clearing up her confusion and restoring her strength.

She wanted a house. Now that she found a purpose in life, Auntie Xiaomei perked up with renewed energy. Rediscovering her mental and physical stamina and her shrewdness, she was more optimistic about her future and became more resolute in taking action. The first thing that came to her mind was the Zhang family. She had followed the lady of the Zhang family as a young servant for thirty long years; there was no reason she should not be recognized as part of the Zhang family. In the new society everybody had equal worth and there was no distinction in stature between mistress and servant. They had absolutely no excuse to exclude her from the Zhang family!

She decided to pay the Zhang family a visit on a Sunday afternoon. As she approached the Zhang residence, however, there was a hesitation in her steps. Before her eyes the bare wall by the small garden was suddenly draped with a lush coat of ivy and the elderly man of the house was arranging pots of azaleas, his grizzled hair next to the pink blooms, and pruning the plants with a pair of shears making a crisp clipping sound. It was she who had helped the elderly Mrs. Zhang tame the philandering

Mr. Zhang, who became well-behaved and discreet, scarcely making a sound when he walked in the house. The thought brought a demure smile to her lips, and then she was jolted back to reality. The azaleas crowned with a cloud of pink blooms vanished, as did the ivy that climbed all over the wall. There were no more clipping sounds from the pruning shears. Only a bare fence wall stood before her, with oleander branches and foliage sticking out of a corner, the flowers long gone and the leaves turned to a tired green. She resumed walking, turning into a back alley, whose cement pavement had fragmented, forming crisscrossing lines woven into an intricate web of foot-tripping cracks. The alley felt narrower than before but the walls at either side of it looked taller, making her claustrophobic. The rays of the afternoon sun passed over the buildings, reached the wall but quickly moved beyond it to throw a yellowish light on the back of the buildings. She watched her own shadow glide along the wall like in a shadow play. The faces and voices she saw and heard through the open back doors along the alley walls were unfamiliar. She made her way toward Number 6 near the end of the alley.

The house of the Zhang family at Number 6 stood out from the rest of the houses. It used to have a frontage of two rooms' width and a height of three stories, like all the other houses in the alley. It was later expanded to include all the land at the end of the alley, on which they built a two-level house with two bedrooms on each floor, across a patio from the original house. She didn't care how many bedrooms there were or how nice they were. She was not greedy; all she asked for was that little eight-square-meter room in which she had stayed for thirty long years. She still remembered with fondness the familiar floral-edged water marks left on its ceiling in the aftermath of several water leakages from the bathroom above.

As she penetrated deep into the narrow

alleyway and got close to Number 6, its door opened, letting out two filthy boys who blew by her like two cyclones, nearly knocking her over. Before she had time to consider whether to chide them, the two boys already hurled over their shoulder an indirect but undisguised profanity at her, bringing a blush to the cheeks of the never-married Auntie Xiaomei, who pretended not to have heard it. Luckily with the door already thrown open, she could sail in unannounced. The place was not the forlorn, quiet house she remembered from her dreams; rather, it was excessively cluttered and noisy with trash-like stuff crammed into the stair landings and the inconsiderate slamming of doors and windows. Her mind strayed once again as she stood outside the kitchen.

The elderly lady of the house slowly descended the staircase and made her way straight to the card table in the living room. If she was missing a fourth player, she would say, "Auntie Xiaomei, come play with us!"

Auntie Xiaomei would sit across from the lady of the house, whose tea-colored dark glasses would reflect the mah-jongg tiles she had before her, thus enabling Auntie Xiaomei to play to her mistress's advantage. Her elderly mistress would say, after winning the game, "Auntie Xiaomei, when you are here, I feel secure and I become smarter." She would reply, "It's because you have a lucky streak today, Mrs. Zhang." The old lady would laugh as her elegant hands typical of the rich shuffled the tiles in a leisurely manner, the tiles making a luxurious sound of "pearls dropped into a jade plate." Just as she was going to laugh with her mistress, the tinkling sound of the bone tiles fell silent, giving way to that of loud footsteps.

It was a girl coming down the stairs. The girl cast a casual glance at her. Before she could ask a question, the girl had walked past her. She steadied her nerves and surveyed the surrounding scenes. She spotted a familiar cupboard painted white standing by the door of a big room and decided that it must be the Zhang family who lived inside that door.

She knocked on the door while taking in the contents of the cupboard. She saw a few piles of clean bowls and a bowl containing a prepared dish of sautéed salted mustard greens and green soy beans and a bowl of cold rice, all arranged neatly although there was a forlorn look to it. As she studied the cupboard, the door opened a crack, about two inches wide. In the gap appeared the pale, gaunt face of the eldest son of the Zhang family, red around the eyes, at the sides of the nose and on the upper lip, signs of a cold. He looked nervous, a humble smile playing on his face. As soon as he recognized Auntie Xiaomei he withdrew the smile and assumed a slightly haughtier air although the nervousness persisted.

"So you are home, Dadi ("oldest younger brother," term of address for a younger male peer)!" she said with a hearty laugh, using a familiar nickname.

Finding no excuse to bar her from the apartment, he let her in.

She walked into the apartment, her hands folded in front of her, hanging coyly. The leaves of the oleander obscured the sun, darkening the room. The door was quietly closed behind her and Dadi came up to her, saying:

"Take a seat, Auntie Xiaomei."

"Dadi, don't be so formal." But she sat down on a vintage sofa, the fringes of its cover frayed, with some strands trailing on the floor while threadbare in other places. This was the sofa her mistress often sat in. She went over the smooth armrest with her hand, trying to feel the residual warmth of the old lady, but instead got a cold sensation at the center of her palm.

"Still working for the Xie family, are you?" Dadi sank into a leather chair opposite her, eyeing her. When she returned his gaze, he averted his eyes.

She turned the question back to him: "Damei ("oldest younger sister"), Xiaomei ("youngest younger sister"), and Xiaodi ("youngest younger brother"), they are all doing well?"

"Xiaodi went to work on a farm in north Jiangsu after graduating from college; Damei is married and lives with her husband's family on Weihaiwei Road; Xiaomei lives at home as she waits for a job assignment." As Dadi updated Auntie Xiaomei, he studied her furtively, but averted his eyes as soon as their eyes met.

"So she has not been sent down to the countryside?" Auntie Xiaomei looked around the room, which contained a full-size bed, under which lay a pair of women's slippers, some kids' toys and a plastic bowl. When she looked back at Dadi after her survey of the room, Dadi immediately turned his eyes away to look at the room that Auntie Xiaomei just finished examining.

"Her health is not very satisfactory, so she is unwilling to go to the countryside."

"And her school didn't insist?"

With a rueful smile Dadi refrained from

explaining, still stealing looks at her.

Auntie Xiaomei was quick to show understanding. "You are in a delicate, awkward position in this matter. You don't want to give the impression you don't want your sister in the house."

He was obviously moved, his eyes reddening some more. But he was now more relaxed and less nervous than before.

Auntie Xiaomei thought to herself, "They must have some ace up their sleeve or some inside track for her to have been able to avoid being sent down to the countryside given their class status." A warning flag went up in her mind.

Dadi left his chair to prepare a cup of tea, which he courteously offered her. He said, "Nowadays no one except you, Auntie Xiaomei, would care to drop in for a visit." As he pronounced the words "Auntie Xiaomei" his voice almost sank to a whimper.

Despite a softening of her heart, Auntie Xiaomei kept a smile on her face. She said, "You are all adults now, fully capable of

taking care of yourselves. You don't really
need Auntie Xiaomei now." She suddenly
recalled how the next generation of the
Zhang family had fired her the very day her
mistress was placed into her coffin. It was a
day like this, sunny outside but dark in the
house. The memory brought tears to her
eyes, but she choked them back.

"Auntie Xiaomei, don't fret over what
happened in the past. Let bygones be
bygones!" As Dadi said this, he hung his head
and darted glances at Auntie Xiaomei.

"At first I was really angry. For a long
time I cursed your callousness and cruelty.
But after a while I didn't feel so bad. On the
contrary I began to feel happy for myself,
realizing that leaving your family when I
did was a blessing in disguise. Now that I
had no more to do with the old lady of the
house, nobody could ever accuse me of any
designs on her. But I am soft-hearted. If
you young people hadn't chased me out of
the house, I wouldn't have had the heart to
leave." Auntie Xiaomei heaved a long sigh

and choked back her tears as she described her feelings at an even pace.

Dadi didn't know how to respond. He kept silent but couldn't keep his inner agitation and emotion down. He felt a strong urge to cry.

"Well, after all is said and done, I am a bleeding heart. I am masochistic. I already told myself I would not worry about you, but I just can't quit worrying. The other day I ran into Granny Xiaohong who lives at Number 3. She says you suffered a lot when the Cultural Revolution started. Your house was turned inside out. Your house was sealed and your belongings hauled away. I fretted night after night, unable to sleep, and only felt better when I thought of your mother. She had had a good life and departed this world early. That was lucky for her because she was spared the pain of witnessing the tragedy. As for you guys, I thought, you could only blame it on fate. Maybe your previous incarnations did not do a good job of perfecting yourselves and

were too superficial or too self-indulgent or
something. But I still couldn't have peace of
mind, so there. I am here today; I have my
self-respect but my feet don't, and it's my
feet that have brought me here."

It was only then that Dadi looked up
and outlined what happened during the
upheaval.

"So they've left you only this room?" she
asked the question thoughtfully.

"There is a smaller room, the one Auntie
used to sleep in, now occupied by my little
sister."

"Show me the room," she said as she got
to her feet.

Although not privy to her motive, Dadi
left his chair and followed her.

When the door of the small room was
pushed open, a damp, cold smell greeted
her. It was a familiar smell. Nothing had
changed except the addition of a few pieces
of furniture, and the replacement of her bed
with a mattress bed for the younger sister.
The water stains on the ceiling, almost the

same as she remembered, had darkened. The window drapes had been half lifted to reveal half of a cistern in the patio, where a woman was brushing something, producing a raspy sound that echoed in the courtyard. She paused to look at the four familiar walls and made her way to the window. She gently lowered the drapes and turned to look intently at Dadi.

Dadi tried to avert his eyes again, but they were trapped by Auntie Xiaomei's determined eyes.

"Dadi, I intend to move back here. My household registration was with the Zhang family for thirty years and I left against my wishes. This room should by right be mine."

Petrified by her eyes, Dadi could only mumble, "Er, how can you say that, Auntie Xiaomei?"

Auntie Xiaomei continued, "If I had come here two years earlier at the height of the Cultural Revolution, to present my claim, who knows how much more I could have gotten out of it. But you know, Dadi, Auntie Xiaomei is not the kind of person to kick someone when he's down. I only come here to discuss this with you when things have calmed down in the past two years."

"Bu-but, there's nothing we can do." Dadi involuntarily took a step backwards.

"You can all stay in the large room and give the small room back to me. The little sister will leave sooner or later when she gets married."

"But the little brother will come home after his stint on the farm." As he said this, Dadi suddenly felt a profound sadness, a sense that they'd been abandoned and each was left to fend for himself, as described by the Chinese phrase "once the tree comes down, all the monkeys scatter and the birds fly off to find their respective new perches." He was on the verge of letting escape an anguished cry.

Auntie Xiaomei looked away, freeing the eyes of Dadi. She said, "I had lived here since the day I came up with your mother from the village. Thirty years I had lived here. It was you who moved me out. I could have raised the matter with the rebel faction of your work unit but then I thought I should first try to resolve it with you. Don't you agree, Dadi?"

His eyes fixed on the face of Auntie Xiaomei, Dadi suddenly plopped down on his knees, swallowing hard and saying with a trembling voice, "Auntie Xiaomei, for mother's sake please have mercy on us!"

This caught Auntie Xiaomei by surprise. Disconcerted, she tried to haul him onto his feet by grabbing his arms but he dodged her, his arms flailing wildly.

"Yes, we were ungrateful, unfeeling, not human to have fired you. We have earned our just deserts for it these past few years. The rebel faction of my work unit came to turn our home upside down, ordered us to crawl on our hands and knees. My wife who was four months pregnant had a miscarriage. The rebel faction from Damei's school dragged us out into the

alley and subjected us to public pillory ..."
He wept bitterly with his hands supporting
his weight on the floor, words failing him
and his head bent lower and lower until it
almost touched the ground.

Watching this man curled in a knot at
her feet, Auntie Xiaomei could no longer
keep back her tears. After all it was she
who had brought him up. She had never
had a baby and he was like her own child
and she poured all the maternal love that
she could imagine into this man. She took
pity on him; but who ever took pity on her?
She wiped off her tears and slowly regained
her composure, letting out a soft sigh. Soon
Dadi calmed down too.

"Frankly, Dadi," she said, "we've all
had a hard life. I went to your maternal
grandmother's home as maid when I was
only thirteen. I saw your mother married
and saw you married but I still don't have a
family of my own. I can't work in someone
else's home until I grow decrepit and die.
I would be too weak to work long before I

die. I couldn't think of any other alternative than to ask for this room back. It was a decision that took me years to make."

"Auntie Xiaomei …" Dadi turned up his face.

Auntie Xiaomei said, "Get on your feet first. I won't listen to you if you stay on your knees."

Dadi said, "I will only stand up after you hear me out. If you refuse to listen I'll refuse to get up."

Finally Dadi yielded to Auntie Xiaomei and got up:

"Auntie Xiaomei, we were too ruthless in the past and we've earned our retribution. If circumstances permit in the future, we will make it up to you, provide for your old age and take care of you to your last days. But in our present circumstances we can barely cope ourselves, with only two rooms, one for me, my wife and my kid, the other for my little sister, and eventually for my little brother, who will be back. He has been sent off to be trained and made stronger. He is certain to come back and will need to live in this room. We really don't have a room to spare."

This toughened Auntie Xiaomei's resolve. "I don't care anymore. Apparently I can't find satisfaction with you. I have to think of other ways then."

"Auntie Xiaomei!" Dadi called after her.

"Don't Auntie Xiaomei me! How much do you really care about your Auntie Xiaomei?" Looking at the gaunt tear-streaked face, she was filled with indignation: this same face had been so cold and haughty at a different time. This memory dispelled all doubt and hesitation. She walked briskly out of the door, slamming it hard. The heavy steel door closed with a loud clang, which triggered a vicious curse:

"Are you tired of living? (a common curse in the local dialect)"

She turned around to see a sleepy face with mucous eyes and driveling mouth sticking out of a second-floor window. She cursed back:

"It's you who are tired of living. Cursing comes natural to you, eh?" With that she hurried off, not wishing to hear an escalated curse.

This was no longer the house that radiated a quiet authority in her memory. Therefore her resolve to move into that house was further firmed. She no longer felt any hesitation. Before the visit she had felt a little intimidated, a little inhibited and a bit ashamed that what she contemplated was an act of desecration. But now she could walk out of the alley with perfect peace of mind.

That was another insomniac night for Auntie Xiaomei. Her action today was only a probe, a reconnaissance mission with a hint of threat, but she had not dealt from a position of strength. Having lived here for almost forty years spanning the old society and the new, she could legitimately claim to be a veteran Shanghainese. She understood that her position was weakened by the fact that her household registration was no longer with the Zhang family, which could easily disown her. That was why she could only deal with the Zhang family to work out a private settlement, because she would never have a case in a court of law. She needed therefore to carefully weigh their relative strengths. Outwardly Dadi was as feckless as a worm. Why else would a man get down on his knees so readily? But on the other hand this could be his secret weapon. A confrontational approach on his part would have been easier to deal with. Auntie Xiaomei repeatedly went over every detail of the day's encounter without being able to conclude who had the upper hand. Now she was wide awake, excited but also so frustrated that her hands and feet felt cold. She wanted to go to sleep but sleep wouldn't come, and she kept trying to fall asleep. Thus she tossed and turned most of the night and when she finally got up in the morning she found everything annoying. Even the couple who employed her was careful not to rub her the wrong way, only whispering behind her back, "What a temper this home attendant has!"

The home attendant working at Number 57 in the same alley as the Xie family dropped in for a visit. Although it took only ten minutes to walk the two blocks separating the two places, they rarely saw each other. Now that the eldest daughter at Number 57 gave birth to a baby boy recently, she could hardly absent herself for a minute. One wondered what excuse she had invented to enable her to get away this time. Although she looked down her nose at the home attendant at Number 57, Auntie Xiaomei was moved by the good will and affection she showed by taking time out of her busy schedule to visit her. She generously treated her guest to a top-quality tea belonging to her employer.

"Jiejie ("Big sister"), are you happy with your work here?" the home attendant of Number 57 asked reverentially, tea cup in her hand.

"See for yourself."

"As I see it, you had it better at the Xie

family. It was so simple and quiet there. Here you always bump into people. How many households live in here anyway?"

"Only two families, but they are large families. In this household there are five, if you include me. The other household has seven members. They have to queue up for a bath in the summer."

"Wouldn't it be nice if you were still with the Xie family? We would be closer and could meet more often."

Every time the Xie family was mentioned she would feel a strong sense of aggrievement, but it was not something she cared to air in front of the home attendant of Number 57. So she said, "It only looks simple and quiet at the Xie place. Outsiders have no idea how annoying it can get."

"Jiejie, you are very particular about things; you can't stand a grain of sand in your eyes! Unlike me. I can settle for less," the home attendant of Number 57 said with lament.

"How have you been? Are you still being

bothered by people from the village?"

This had the effect of causing the eyes of the home attendant of Number 57 to redden. "If I tell you, you will say I'm masochistic to allow myself to be used like this. The balance in my savings account hasn't grown by one cent since last you were there."

Auntie Xiaomei couldn't refrain from pounding on the table with her fist as she said, "It's time you kick out this adopted son of yours. What's so terrible about not having a son? You would not be the only one without a son."

"What will I do when I am too old to work? I've taken all this abuse in the interest of being provided for in my old age."

"When you return to your village a poor woman, you think your adopted son would take you in? Even if you want to make preparations for your old age, you shouldn't loosen your purse strings this early in the game. Look at it this way. If you have money, you can live anywhere; you don't even need to go back to the village. Doesn't your Xiaoshushu ("younger brother of husband") own a house?" At this point her heart gave a sudden start and began racing, and her cheeks burned. She made an effort to calm herself before continuing in an even tone, "You have such a special relationship between you. Why can't you live there in your old age?"

Large patches of color rose in Number 57's face; she said, directing a "pshaw" at the floor, "It's his house. What does it have to do with me?"

"I just mentioned it in passing. Look how agitated you got!" Auntie Xiaomei said dismissively, with a laugh.

Number 57 also laughed, the blush remaining on her cheeks.

Auntie Xiaomei shot her a glance, saying, "Tell Jiejie the truth. Have you done the despicable thing with him again?"

Number 57 made to hit her with her fist; she dodged. After a while Auntie Xiaomei heaved a sigh and said:

"When there was trouble, you came to

me asking Jiejie to get you out of trouble. Now that it blew over, you don't tell me anything anymore."

"My dear Jiejie, you know how delicate this thing is. I couldn't very well shout it from the rooftop! It's nothing to be proud of. I don't want to hear people call me a slut. I told you everything because we were like sisters, but you had no right to make fun of me like that." She wiped at her eyes.

Auntie Xiaomei turned serious and said with sincerity, "Did I mean you any harm when I asked the question? Do you see a third person here? This incident of yours happened such a long time ago. Have you heard anything recently?"

Number 57 shook her head.

"Sometimes I really feel sorry for you. That fetus in your womb was your own and you had it removed. And you give your money away to an adopted son. All because that fetus was considered illegitimate and couldn't be explained to people. You could have braved public opinion and thrown the question of illegitimacy to the winds. It was conceived by you and therefore was yours. But would we dare? We wouldn't."

Number 57 had by now melted into tears, sobbing uncontrollably.

"There, there, let's not talk about these hurtful things. I'll get a hot towel for you. Wash your face and go home. Otherwise the lady of your house will complain." She left her chair to pour hot water into a basin and lent her own towel to Number 57.

Overwhelmed by this honor, Number 57 stopped crying, not wanting to squander the good will of Auntie Xiaomei. She suppressed her sobs, washed her face and hurried off.

Watching from the window, Auntie Xiaomei saw her emerge from the lobby of the building and merge into the bustling crowd, weaving through it, jostling and being jostled, finally disappearing in it.

She thought, her Xiaoshushu owns a house! And the thought haunted her. As she rinsed the rice, put it in the cooker, prepared the dishes, sat eating, did the dishes and finally went to bed, a voice would whisper to her, "her Xiaoshushu owns a house." Lying in the room made naked by the streetlamp and the moonlight, her ears filled with the sound of the rise and fall of the kids' breathing, she made her calculations: Sooner or later her Xiaoshushu will retire, and when that happens—of course she couldn't leave Number 57 out, not Auntie Xiaomei, she was not that kind of ungrateful person. She envisioned lovingly life in that little house with Number 57. She pictured a cosy little house, and remembered all the pleasant traits in Number 57's temperament. Even if she failed to get into the Zhang house, she would have the house in Zhabei as a backup, a fallback. She reckoned that as long as one put one's mind to it and used one's head, one would find opportunities open up before one's eyes. The thought put her in a more upbeat frame of mind, but the seduction of a bright future disturbed her inner peace and her sleep. She would lie awake all night until it was day, and during the day she would be sleepy and looked forward to bedtime. Maybe she was—the thought was depressing—too old. The days when she burst with energy were no more. And that made the quest for a place of her own even more urgent.

Now she pursued a two-track approach. She would not give up on that room in the Zhang house; she went there every Sunday to press her claim. Faced with her offensive, Dadi, his face bathed in tears, would fall back and ask for quarter. She had a confrontation with the little sister on two occasions. The little sister was tougher than Dadi but whenever she spoke up Dadi would yell at her to keep quiet. She would ignore him and continue to argue with Auntie Xiaomei. But she was after all too young, too unsophisticated in the face of Auntie Xiaomei, who dismissed her as a rival to worry about after a few skirmishes. She came away every time feeling like a triumphant general, the clear winner of the verbal argument. But on the way home she began to have an uneasy feeling; she was not getting any traction—the house remained in the hands of the Zhang family and her household registration remained with the family for whom she worked. Every time she went in the Zhang house only to leave it again, the prospect of going in and staying for good remained elusive as ever. Only then did she realize the lethal power packed by the sniveling softness of Dadi's tactic. This only provoked her to greater anger and bolstered her fighting will. As this was going on she also increased her contact with Number 57, cultivating closer ties with her. Finally one day Number 57 took a half day off and invited Auntie Xiaomei to accompany her to her Xiaoshushu's house in Zhabei to celebrate his fiftieth birthday. Auntie Xiaomei accepted the invitation after putting up only token resistance.

That afternoon the home attendant of Number 57, clad in a brand new side-lapel hydron blue blouse and her hair slicked

back behind her ears, came bouncing and
swaying to fetch Auntie Xiaomei, who
briefly arranged her dress and picked up
a cotton mesh bag before leaving with
Number 57. They changed buses twice. As
they traveled further, the cars on the road
thinned and the buildings at the roadside
shrank in height until they became one-
level structures. The road widened but
became quieter. As the bus door opened
and closed to let passengers on and off, the
people looked and sounded different. The
subei (north Jiangsu) dialect seemed to be
the predominant language. One had the
sense of having left Shanghai and arrived
in a completely different place. Even Auntie
Xiaomei, who had lived in Shanghai for
the past forty years, was humbled to find
out how much she didn't know about the
city. But on the other hand she also felt a
superiority to this community and couldn't
help betraying a disdain in her face and
an iciness in her eyes as she surveyed the
surroundings.

After they got off the bus, they crossed a street as wide as a highway and walked some way before making a turn. There the street sharply narrowed, making it difficult to walk two abreast, so they formed a single file. Under the eaves that hung low to almost touch one's shoulders, people sat and talked. Taking barely a few steps on the cobblestone pavement of the narrow street, Auntie Xiaomei felt a pain grow in the plant of her foot that reminded her of that associated with corn growths. They emerged from the narrow street into an intersection, an open space with a public faucet standing in its middle, its water left running and women sitting around it rubbing their clothes on their washboards. When they were done washing, they tilted the wooden washbasins to empty them, the grayish sudsy water running down the pavement, right by the shoes of Auntie Xiaomei, who hastened to dodge it, to finally find its resting place in a shallow culvert. Already a light perspiration broke out as Auntie Xiaomei desperately tried to get out of the way of the dirty water. She was angry but didn't want to linger where she was a total stranger. Number 57 walked briskly ahead and if Auntie Xiaomei had slowed down she'd have easily lost sight of her, so she hurried to catch up, resenting it all the way. When Number 57 paused in her fast march and Auntie Xiaomei finally caught up with her, Xiaoshushu appeared at a wooden door, making it impossible for Auntie Xiaomei to vent her frustration on Number 57.

Number 57 said, briefly stamping her feet, "What annoyance! That was a tiresome trip. The buses were so crowded. I'm exhausted."

Standing to one side, Auntie Xiaomei thought, "This is not the first time you've made this trip. The buses were not that crowded either. Why did you walk so fast if you were exhausted?" But she kept a smile on her face, unobtrusively sizing up Xiaoshushu.

Xiaoshushu looked more like a Dabaibai (older brother of husband). He was fifty but he had the appearance of someone who was sixty, his face creased with deeply chiseled wrinkles and the skin on his hands coarse as bark. But a closer look would reveal a lean and mean body with strong bone, no flab, and no useless muscle. He wore a denim overall directly over his sweat shirt and a work hat, with tufts of hoary hair sticking out from under it. As she studied him, her mind strayed to what happened between him and Number 57 and her cheeks burned for no good reason. She cursed herself for it, "Dirty mind!"

"Very kind of you, very kind of you!" He asked them in.

Once inside their eyes had to adjust before they could see in the darkened room. It was a one-level sixteen- or seventeen-square-meter house in the local style, its bricked floor hiding encrusted dirt and filth that could never be cleaned out. The whitewashed walls had been blackened by soot and covered with layers of posters used solely as wallpaper and therefore juxtaposed in a haphazard manner: Zhu Yingtai (protagonist of a legendary love story) next to the white legs of a chubby baby, oil workers side by side with the Cowherd and the Weaver Girl (figures in ancient Chinese folklore). The furniture consisted of a plank bed with a roll of light-weight blanket on top and a yellowed mosquito net hanging above, a bare wood chest of drawers, a square table, a few square stools and a bamboo chair. A desk with drawers missing a leg stood against the wall in a corner. On it sat a kerosene lamp and a small cabinet for chinaware and above it was a square recess cut into the wall that served as a rack for bottles of oil, soy sauce, salt and vinegar. After a cursory glance around the house, Auntie Xiaomei was disappointed. She certainly had not thought that a relative of Number 57's would live in a house of any luxury, but she definitely was unprepared for such a modest dwelling.

Disappointment accentuated her fatigue; she sank into a bamboo chair, putting a foot up on the other knee and starting to rub the ankle wrapped in a snow white nylon sock.

At the urging of Number 57, Xiaoshushu went to fetch tea and some cups. Number 57 disapproved of the cups, finding them dirty, so off went Xiaoshushu to wash them. It came to Auntie Xiaomei's attention that the water used to rinse the cups was drawn from a wooden pail. She reckoned that the water must have been hauled from the public faucet she had passed on her way here. From tap water her thought turned to the toilet. Then she realized that the plank bed was not flush against the wall and a printed cloth curtain had been drawn over the gap between the bed and the wall. That must be the toilet. As she studied the setup, Number 57 reverentially handed her a cup of tea.

"Jiejie, have some tea."

"I'm so sorry, if only I had known you were coming …" Xiaoshushu added.

Before she had time to react, Number 57 forestalled Auntie Xiaomei by saying, to Xiaoshushu, "You talk too much. Bring me the fish you bought. I'll butcher it for you."

Xiaoshushu went off to get the fish, obviously pleased and running with an exaggerated bob. Once she had the fish in her hand, Number 57 yelled:

"The cleaver!"

Off he went again, a bounce in his steps, to get the cleaver.

Viewing their busy minuet with scorn, Auntie Xiaomei nonetheless said, "What can I do to help?"

Number 57, motioning her to sit down with a nudge of her elbow, said, "Don't you move. The birthday celebration was just an excuse to invite you to dinner. So you are the honored guest today. I know you are used to good food but for a change you can try our simpler fare today."

Auntie Xiaomei sat back down, thinking with an inward sneer, "So now it's already 'our' this and 'our' that!"

It was getting dark outside and darker still in the house. Number 57 let out a squeak, "The lights!" And the lights were turned on. Xiaoshushu, squatting right behind her, was at the ready to carry out any command that might be issued by her. To see Number 57 exercise a rare authority gave Auntie Xiaomei gooseflesh and a taste of sour grapes. She cursed in her mind, "I am the honored guest, my foot! You just wanted to show me how you had the man under your thumb. How unseemly you are!" She slowly and primly sipped her tea, betraying no emotion.

Number 57 busied herself with all that cooking entailed and finally laid out a rich array of dishes on the table. Her face was flushed with exertion, her hair sticking out at the ears in fluffy tufts and she moved about with crispness and celerity. She was a changed person. It was pitch-dark outside now. Behind closed doors, it was dinner time for all families and the daytime bustle and noise had died down. The cobblestone street meandered away toward the sapphire night sky in the distance. All was quiet, a different kind of quiet. It had a soothing effect on Auntie Xiaomei, who was slowly regaining her inner peace.

A dull light, hung over the piping hot feast spread out on the table. At the insistence of the brother-in-law and the sister-in-law, Auntie Xiaomei downed a cup of rice wine, which lit a fire in her body and her heart, making her slightly light-headed. Through a mist in her eyes she took another look around her. The interior of the small house behind the teary veil gave her a cosy feeling. She moved her chopsticks in slow motion and took another look about the house. She thought: The important thing is to have a place of one's own. It's up to you to make a house beautiful or an eyesore out of it. What do men know about homemaking? They'd make the nicest villa into a pigsty. With work, this house could be made presentable she was. So engrossed in these reflections, that she was unaware of the feverish foot nudging under the table.

When they left the house, the sky was already studded with stars. Auntie Xiaomei marveled at the brilliance of the stars and the height and profundity of the sky. After contemplating the sky for a short while, she strode off.

Both had had some wine and each had her own private reason to feel contented. The buoyant mood of both brought them closer on their way home. They walked arm in arm. Number 57 talked in her incessant volubility about everything that had to do with her Xiaoshushu. Auntie Xiaomei listened with interest and finally asked slowly:

"When your Xiaoshushu retires, will he be going back to his village?"

This had the effect of instantly silencing Number 57, who said after a pause, "Where else could he go when he retires?"

"He can retire in Shanghai. He does have a house in the city," she said in a soft voice, her heart giving a lurch at the word "house."

"You think his woman would allow that to happen? And you think he would abandon those parasites of his?" Number 57 said with sudden anger, her voice rising.

"You are right. As things are, he is no longer his own man," Auntie Xiaomei said with sympathy.

"He is a man. He makes his own decisions. He can do anything, unlike unlucky me. I have no children of my own." Tears brimmed in her eyes as she gnashed her teeth.

"There! There!" Auntie Xiaomei said soothingly, "What's wrong with being single? You have less aggravation. See? I am single too and I don't moan and lament."

"Jiejie, you are strong. I am different. I am too guileless and too pliant."

"Let's keep each other company when we retire!" Auntie Xiaomei said in jest. But Number 57 took it seriously.

"Jiejie, do you mean it?"

"When have I ever lied?" she retorted

flippantly, making it sound even more like a falsehood. Number 57's distress increased.

"Jiejie, seriously, if we could keep each other company in old age, I would feel so much more reassured."

"It would be nice to keep each other's company, but where can two homeless ladies live? Who would take in two old ladies who have lost the ability to work?"

"We'll find a place."

"A place? It's easy for you to say. Shanghai is not like your village. It would be easier to find gold in the street than to find a place to live in the city."

"We'll take over his house," she said angrily. "Let that son of a bitch go back to his house in the village. Let those parasites of his eat him alive."

Once again Auntie Xiaomei's heart gave a lurch. The alcohol was out of her system now and she sobered up all of a sudden, the dregs having settled to the bottom of her mind. That Number 57 would say something like this of her own accord was both surprising and expected. There was a long pensive pause because she was considering how to respond. She must not appear too eager, which would scare her off; nor could she afford not to give a reply, thus letting her off the hook. As she mulled over the right response, Number 57 said in great anxiety:

"Seriously, Jiejie, what do you think of my idea?"

That convinced Auntie Xiaomei, who said with deliberation, "I appreciate your devotion to me. But your Xiaoshushu may not go along."

"He won't dare say no!" Number 57 had a sudden burst of self-confidence.

"Of course you are in-laws, you are family, but this is not just anything, it is a house we are talking about," she added.

"I'll go talk to him day after tomorrow when I find some free time." Number 57's mind had been made up.

The bus entered the city, the stars in the night sky now dimmed in contrast to the twinkling streetlamps whose light reflected off the asphalt pavement creating a gleam on its surface. They walked off the bus, hand in hand, shivering as a cold breeze blew their way.

Since their return from Zhabei, Auntie Xiaomei felt reassured. Her battle goal remained the small room in the Zhang house, with the house in Zhabei serving as a fallback position. Although far short of her ideal of a house for her retirement, the Zhabei house was perfectly fine as a backup. With this fallback plan, she could now forge ahead fearlessly. Her energy had been recharged.

She fetched one of the trunks stored with the Xie family to the Zhang house and deposited it in the small room. A dejected Dadi followed her into the room, looking defenseless against the assault. But the next time she went there, she found the trunk placed outside the door, and the door had been locked. Dadi said there was nothing he could do about it; it was his little sister

who had locked it and taken the key with
her. His sister had a lousy temper; she
wouldn't even listen to her older brother.
Auntie Xiaomei demanded to pry off the
lock. Dadi went to get the tools for her: a
hammer and a screwdriver. Once she had
the tools in her hands, she didn't know
what to do with them. Angrily she threw
the tools down and walked away. Worried
about the trunk, she turned around midway
and was going to take the trunk to the large
room when she realized it had also been
locked and Dadi was nowhere to be found.
She had no alternative but to knock on the
neighbor's door. Despites fears of being
snubbed, she hoped to get them to agree
to the temporary safekeeping of her trunk.
The man who opened the door was dressed
like a workman. He had a nice manner and
asked who she was, what the story was about
the trunk. In a rage she poured out all her
grievances. After hearing her out, the man
became even more solicitous. He asked
her in, invited her to sit down and delved

deeper. This alarmed her and she became more reticent. As soon as she stopped volunteering more details, the man said, "These bourgeois sons of bitches! They are unscrupulous!" This rather grated on her ears and she didn't want to stay, regretting having already divluged too much. She could see that this man did not move in the same circles as either she or the Zhang family. But the man added, "You wouldn't get anywhere if you continued doing it your way."

He sounded as if he was going to offer a suggestion on how to proceed, so she sat back down.

"You take your household registration to the police station and ask them to enter you in the Zhang family's book," he said.

"But I have no way of getting hold of the Zhang family's book of household registrations!"

"File a complaint with the police. Times have changed. How can the bourgeois sons of bitches still think they could lord it over the poor? When the police talk to those guys, they will behave," he explained to her patiently.

She started paying visits to the police station, but they were less enthusiastic than the man who suggested the approach. The police asked her, "What's your relationship to the Zhang family?"

She told them the truth.

"No way. What era do you think we are in? How can people still employ servants?" They immediately shot it down.

She hastened to explain that it had nothing to do with employment. All she asked for was a room.

The policeman knit his brows, becoming impatient. She shouldn't even think about what she was thinking about at a time when the government was cracking down on the "apartment grab." Perish the thought, they lectured her.

She then went on to give a detailed explanation about her special relationship to the Zhang family in order to dispel any suspicion of an "apartment grab." They were willing to hear her out, but said at the end of her story, "You are no longer working in the Zhang family, so it will be difficult."

She made her way home, feeling bitter. That room in the Zhang house was receding farther and farther away. The ground seemed to shake under her, making her unsteady and disoriented. She felt like in a dream. Decidedly she was a pale shadow of her former self. She used to be able to accomplish anything she set out to do. Didn't she have the Zhangs and the Xies in the palm of her hand? But in the end she was out in the street, all alone. Suddenly she found herself laughable. After all neither of those places was her own home. Without a home, she had no place, no standing in society; and no matter how strong or resourceful she was, she would not be able to bring her talents to full bloom. It seemed a bit late to realize this truth only at her age. But she was not going to admit defeat. There was still that house in Zhabei as a fallback. At the thought, she felt somewhat reassured. She set off again after composing herself.

She did her best to encourage Number 57 to make frequent visits to Zhabei. If Number 57 couldn't find time in the day, Auntie Xiaomei would urge her to go in the evening. As long as she came back first thing in the morning, her employer would have no cause to complain. As for groceries, Auntie Xiaomei would get them for her on her own daily errand and Number 57 could pick them up on her way home. It would be a short side trip for Number 57 after she got off the bus. Auntie Xiaomei always kept the freshest for Number 57. When she bought two portions of pork thigh, she would leave the one from the hind leg with less bone for Number 57. She would keep meat with more fat for herself while leaving the leaner meat for Number 57. That way the lady of the house at Number 57 would be embarrassed to raise any serious objections. On one such morning, Number 57 came to Auntie

Xiaomei. She appeared to be in a hurry. Her
hair was ragged, her cheeks were flushed
and there were dark rings around her eyes.
She turned to leave as soon as she picked up
the groceries. Auntie Xiaomei took a step
after her and cautioned, "Don't get muddle-
headed. If you do, I'll wash my hands of
you!" Number 57 spat and left in a hurry.
Once, Number 57 told her after getting back
from Zhabei, "The son of a gun agreed. The
household registration can be transferred
any time." The next time she reported,
"The son of a gun reneged. Someone must
have talked nonsense into him." Then
he agreed again. It was a seesaw and one
could never be sure what he would end up
deciding. Auntie Xiaomei was not unduly
worried, because she was in the middle of a
protracted war with the Zhang family. The
winner hadn't been declared and she was
not in possession of any reliable, tangible
proof but she wasn't giving up hope just yet.
She would actually be in a bit of a quandary
if at this moment the Zhabei house had

become available. She abandoned that fight
only when she learned that Dadi of the
Zhang family had, through his connections
successfully split the household into two
independent ones: one composed of himself,
his wife and children living in the large
room and another composed of his little
sister and little brother sharing the small
room. Neither the housing administration,
nor the police, nor even the rebel factions
had any grounds for denying a room to a
household. Auntie Xiaomei finally realized
the ace up Dadi's sleeve and the reason
his little sister had been spared the fate of
being sent to the countryside. Although the
Zhang family had fallen into the dust and
had been swept into the ashcan of history,
they had to be allowed a living space, be
it only in a crack or a loophole, as long as
society still upheld their right to existence.
What Auntie Xiaomei failed to understand
was who had passed down to the younger
generation of the Zhang family this kind of
astuteness and skill of maneuver, given that

the late elder lady of the house was so weak-willed and the elder man of the house was good at nothing except philandering and debauchery. Perhaps they had atavistically inherited the qualities of the generation before their parents, the generation that founded the family business. Or they had got it from Auntie Xiaomei.

Now she had only one option left, the fallback pushed to the forefront. Without another fallback, she had to stake all on a single throw.

She didn't know how to kill such a long night in a room made naked by the moon and the streetlamps. She couldn't close her eyes with light weighing on her eyelids. The children's snoring interfered with her thoughts. So many things crowded on her mind, diffused and out of focus. In this most serene of nights she was least at peace, her mind abuzz with thoughts about the past and the future, forming a jumble that blurred into a blank whenever she tried to tease out the tangled threads, leaving only the duet of the two children's snoring, alternating between them like a pendulum.

She decided she needed to personally lead the charge on the Zhabei front.

On a day of rest at Xiaoshushu's factory, Auntie Xiaomei changed into a neat dress and headed to Zhabei, a box of *saqima* (honeyed Chinese noodle cake) in her cotton knit mesh bag. She got off one bus, transferred to another and she began to see more wide open spaces and hear the Subei (north Jiangsu) dialect spoken in louder tones and with greater conviction. Auntie Xiaomei rocked and swayed with the lurching bus; as the landscape outside the window emptied of buildings, a forlorn, vacuous feeling took hold of her. The sun, brilliant to a fault, dazzled and disconcerted her. She got off the bus, walked a short distance on the highway-like street before turning into a side street as narrow as an alley. The sun's rays hit the cobblestone pavement with unmitigated intensity, sending reflected glare in all directions off every stone, dazzling her eyes. She strode over the gleaming stones. In the noon hours, the streets were deserted; not properly shut off, the public faucet standing near the intersection dripped, the droplets of water splashing into a fine mist as they hit the concrete with a ticktack sound.

She almost didn't recognize the house; it was so small and squat, nearly buried by the two neighboring houses, abjectly occupying a shaky toehold, its wooden door leaving gaps of two fingers' width both at its top and at its bottom. After a pause at the door, she finally decided to knock when she saw the address plate nailed onto the door. There was no response; she knocked again. This time a tentative, indistinct voice was heard behind the door, sounding like "Who is it?" Not knowing how to answer that question, she repeated the knock.

As the door opened, a sleepy-eyed Xiaoshushu appeared, and when he recognized Auntie Xiaomei, he got into a fluster, hastening to invite her in, but with a slight hesitation, which did not stop Auntie Xiaomei from letting herself in. The bed was unmade, a smell of scallion-flavored flatulence almost caused Auntie Xiaomei to cover up her nose, but she refrained from doing it, saying with a bright smile:

"Xiaoshushu! Not going out on your day of rest? I was passing by and thought I would pay a little visit to Xiaoshushu."

"I see. I was wondering what wind had blown Auntie Xiaomei this way. Very kind of you, very kind of you." He stood there, unsure whether he should go and make his bed first.

Auntie Xiaomei drew a stool and sat down without being asked. She said, "Can I trouble you to pour me a glass of water? It was a tiring walk and I need a drink of water and to rest my poor feet."

Thankfully given an errand, Xiaoshushu ran off quickly to get her some tea. He had heard a lot about this Auntie Xiaomei from his sister-in-law and felt greatly indebted to her. He had been momentarily at a loss as to how to show that gratitude.

"Does Xiaoshushu cook his own meals or eat at the cafeteria?" Auntie Xiaomei asked with deliberation as she savored her tea.

"I eat in the cafeteria when I work, but I cook after work." He sat down on a stool and answered her question unhurriedly.

"You cook on a coal brazier?"

"No, I use a kerosene stove."

"Oh, no wonder your sister-in-law has been asking me for daily necessities ration coupons to trade for kerosene coupons."

"She's always coming to you for help. I'm very grateful." He was becoming more fluent and occasionally came up with inspired, shrewd words.

"We are like sisters. I am the only one she can turn to for help." Setting down her cup and briefly arranging her hair, she took out the box of pastry from the mesh bag and casually placed it on the table.

Xiaoshushu asked, rising from his chair, "What is this? I can't ... You put me to shame."

"It's only a small gift. You are putting me to shame if you don't accept it."

"No, no, you must take it home with you, Auntie Xiaomei."

"Don't make a fuss over an insignificant gift like this. Relax." And her hand pressed down on the box, as if grinding it into the tabletop, immobilizing it. Xiaoshushu was reduced to rubbing his hands, saying:

"Very kind of you, very kind of you!" But at heart he knew very well this was a prelude to what Auntie Xiaomei was going to say next. He could only half guess what she was going to say.

Auntie Xiaomei picked up her cup and savored the tea. Xiaoshushu watched intently the mouth sipping the tea, waiting for the shoe to drop. Finally she set down her cup and, to his surprise, asked:

"Do you also use the kerosene stove to boil water? Doesn't kerosene cost a lot of money?"

"There is a *laohuzao* (literally 'tiger stove') near by that sells hot drinking water.

I get my hot drinking water from them."

"That's better." Then she fell silent.

"Jiejie, you were visiting a friend in this neighborhood?" Xiaoshushu asked.

"I had to take care of something. I was passing through."

"How is my sister-in-law?"

"If you want her to come see you, I'll pass on the message when I get back. It's no trouble at all."

"That's not what I mean. Not at all." A little embarrassed, Xiaoshushu smoothed his crew-cut hair with the palm of his hand.

"Your sister-in-law has a hard life. You should be kind to her." Auntie Xiaomei exhorted with empathy.

"Yes, yes. My older brother died so young."

Auntie Xiaomei took another draught of tea before putting the cup down. He looked up at her, waiting for her to speak. He wished she would just out with it; that way he would no longer be kept in suspense. He was certain she'd come with a mission. But she rose to her feet and said:

"I'm well rested and had my tea. It's time to leave."

After all the suspense, nothing happened! It was almost a letdown, but Xiaoshushu was relieved.

At the door, Auntie Xiaomei paused and said over her shoulder, "Oh, by the way, did your sister-in-law mention that matter to you?"

"What matter?" He started, his relaxed nerves instantly tautened.

"The matter about your retiring to your native village and us taking care of this house for you."

"She did mention it." Caught unprepared, he blurted out the answer.

"Seriously, think about it. Letting us stay in it beats leaving it vacant and locked up. You'll remain the owner and the household head. We will just be using it. What do you think?"

"Auntie Xiaomei is very thoughtful" was

the only answer he could muster.

"We can rent it from you and pay a monthly rent, Xiaoshushu." Auntie Xiaomei, with a smile playing on her face, said it, half seriously.

"Auntie Xiaomei, now you are joking." Beads of perspiration formed on the forehead of Xiaoshushu.

"I'm not joking. As the saying goes, even blood brothers should settle their accounts to the last cent." Auntie Xiaomei studied him with a smile.

"We'll have occasion to talk about money, but …" He scratched his head with the extra short hair, making a rustling sound.

"But what?"

"You move in only after I retire, right?"

"Naturally. We've been talking only about what happens after you retire. I wouldn't come if you invited me to live here now. It's too quiet and too far from downtown and so inconvenient to everything."

"True, true."

"But our household registration can be

transferred here first."

"There's no hurry for that. No hurry."

"No hurry now, yes. But things have to be set in motion. I hate leaving things to the last moment when there will be great confusion."

"Yes, yes." Put on the defensive, Xiaoshushu ran out of ideas and was reduced to parrying Auntie Xiaomei's thrusts the best he could.

"All right, I'm off now. I'll tell your sister-in-law to come this evening." Auntie Xiaomei realized that she mustn't press him too hard under the circumstance and it was time to quit while she was ahead. She emerged from the narrow street into the square at the intersection, where the public faucet had been turned full-throttle to wash a bed sheet. Droplets of water scattered in all directions; some fell on the topside of her feet clad in square-toed cloth shoes, sending up a cool sensation. She walked on.

The bus slowly weaved its way through the bustling, noisy downtown. Off the bus, the huge crowds, like tidal waves, carried her in unwanted directions. It was some time before she fought her way across the street and made it to the alley where Number 57 worked. She told Number 57 to go to Zhabei that night because her Xiaoshushu wanted to see her about something. Then she slowly walked back to her own building. She believed that with the groundwork laid by her that day and the pleasures Number 57 could offer in bed, the matter was eighty to ninety percent sewed up. Although never married and having no personal experience of the thing between man and woman, she didn't need to go to school to know what it could do.

Having lost the battle with the Zhang family, she devoted her mind exclusively to the house in Zhabei. Every month or every other month, she would visit Zhabei with Number 57. They'd bring groceries and rustle up a meal on the kerosene stove, to the intense delight of Xiaoshushu, who, they hoped, would be more disposed to agree to anything they asked after being pampered like this. Auntie Xiaomei seized on the opportunity to mention the matter of transferring their household registration to the house and he said, "The matter is a done deal. Sooner or later your household registration will be transferred. On my honor as a man, I swear I will not renege." Having lost her head after all the sweet talk and promises of her Xiaoshushu, Number 57 echoed his opinion, "Jiejie, have a little patience. If he dared to renege, I would personally behead him." She hit his nape with the side of her palm and he drew in his head in perfect coordination.

Sitting in the dark, outside the illuminated region of the room, Auntie Xiaomei watched silently the banter between the brother-in-law and sister-in-law. She felt a little lost, a little humiliated, a little bitter and a bit worried. She didn't want to think, didn't dare to think about anything lest she should burst out crying. She sat quietly, with her hands folded coyly in her lap. Her face veiled in the shade cast by the lamp, a gilded edge along the contours of her head and shoulders, she sat stock still, as solemn and stately as a statue of Guanyin (the goddess of mercy).

They were ten years from the retirement of Xiaoshushu. Auntie Xiaomei was determined to wait for ten years and work hard in those ten years, until the day of the move-in. Her yearning for that day had become so intense she no longer had the courage to dream about it. She stopped thinking so far ahead but lived one day, one month at a time, working away, incrementally approaching the day when she could finally move into that house. The ten-year-long journey to that house would require patience and perseverance on Auntie Xiaomei's part, in addition to her innate shrewdness. Step after resolute step she plodded on until, in the fifth year, glimmers of hope began to flicker. In an equal number of years, with effort, the house would be in her reach.

No one had seen it coming, but, with the overthrow of the Gang of Four, the "succession" system was restored. Taking advantage of the system, Xiaoshushu opted for early retirement and the third child of his parents in his native village, a dolt of a north Jiangsu rustic, succeeded him in his job at the factory, moving his household registration to the house, becoming its lawful and legitimate owner. There he would get married, have children and children's children, who would take over the house when their respective turn came.

Auntie Xiaomei fell gravely ill and as she lay in her bed she reviewed every detail of her life. She thought, when she was still a servant in the Zhang family, it should have occurred to her that the elderly Mrs. Zhang would one day pass from the scene and she shouldn't have insisted on playing tough and should have ingratiated herself more with the younger generation of the Zhangs. Since she did insist on playing tough, she should have stuck to her toughness to the end and refused to leave or to transfer her household registration out. Since she finally did leave for the sake of self-respect, she should have found a husband for herself. Failing that, she should have taken advantage of the start of the Cultural Revolution to join the "apartment grab" to snatch an apartment for herself instead of being so civilized and restrained by scruples. Failing all of the above, she should have taken her house registration to Xiaoshushu when he was in an excellent mood and insisted on transferring it to his house then and there. If he had refused, she could have denounced him for having taken sexual advantage of his widowed sister-in-law ... Her failure lay in her inability to resolutely choose between virtue and evil and therefore she was neither unscrupulous enough nor virtuous enough. She was bold and resourceful yet lacked strategic vision. But no matter how shrewd Auntie Xiaomei was, could she have bucked the tide of the times? No

matter how tough Auntie Xiaomei was,
fate always proved tougher.

Ah Fang's Light

There are times when people feel downcast, just as there are days of gloomy weather.

Along the rain-drenched side street, the doors were tightly closed. The pitter patter of raindrops on the road surface echoed in the quiet of the deserted street. The sight of the leaden shroud of clouds and the monotonous sound of the rain brought on an undefinable depression.

On days of bright sunshine this little street is not without its charm. Outside the half open doors, old folks pick over the vegetables for the day's meals and the

children play boisterously. Behind the
quiet, sedate old folks and the loud, lively
children are their respective homes. What
kind of lives do people live in these houses
facing the street? One is curious to know.
That is, if one has time, and attention, to
spare.

One day, one very ordinary day, neither
overcast nor cloudless, as I walked through
the neighborhood and happened to look
over my shoulder, I saw, inside a wide
open door, a messy table left uncleared,
although it was well past lunch time, and
a stocky man stretched out on a bamboo
cot, fast asleep, a fly parked imperturbably
on his jowl. An old woman, probably the
man's mother, operated a clunky sewing
machine, whose rough sound drowned
out the man's snoring. The room was filled
with nondescript objects that could more
properly be called trash and a fetid odor
originating from the house assailed my
nostrils. I quickly turned my head about
and walked on under the spotted shade of

the Chinese parasol trees, on whose leaves
the setting sun cast a golden hue.

When I moved into my new home later,
I would pass through this street three times
a day on my way to work. As time went on,
a small fruit stand appeared one day under
a window facing the street. The window
and the door were newly painted a reddish
brown, both overhung with a wide, green
fiberglass awning to provide shelter against
rain. Beside the stand sat a girl with a
Japanese doll-style haircut, the dense bangs
falling over her lively eyes, framing a clean-
featured face a bit on the pale side accented
by a pair of naturally rosy, supple lips. Clad
in a red dress, she sat, like a hovering red
cloud, by the yellow pears, green apples
and black water chestnuts, quietly reading
a picture storybook or knitting a woolen
sweater boasting more colors than merely
red. When someone walked by, she would
raise her eyes, half-hidden behind her
silken, black bangs. If the passer-by slowed
down, she would rise from her chair, quiet

but expectant. Her expectant look rarely went unrewarded.

On one occasion I paused before her fruit stand. She came up to me and said, "Can I sell you something?" The coarse, hoarse voice was sharply at odds with her clean, winsome features. Failing to get an immediate response, and therefore believing I was vacillating, she added, "Today's honeydew melons are very good. They were unloaded at the Shiliupu wharf only last night. You pay a higher price for them but you get your money's worth."

I didn't get any honeydew melon but picked a few apples. I could see that the hands manipulating the scale were quite large, with thick knuckles and dried, wizened palms, silent witnesses to long years of hard menial work. In contrast her face was young, with smooth, finely textured and fair-complexioned cheeks and deep, clear eyes. After weighing the apples, she computed the price on a very small calculator with her thick finger punching on buttons the size of a rice kernel, generously waiving the small change in the price displayed on the device. She helped me put the apples in my book bag.

After dark, business would pick up considerably and a man would join the girl to tend the stand. He called her Ah Fang. I presumed the man was her husband, although she was, I thought, really too young to have a husband. But one day I was suddenly aware of a change in Ah Fang. After passing in front of the stand a few times and paying closer attention, I finally noticed an enlargement of her girth, a clear sign of pregnancy. The realization gave rise to a curious, mixed feeling in me. On the one hand I found it a pity; on the other hand I was moved. As a matter of fact, when I gave the matter further thought, I found them to be a very nice match: he was stocky and solidly built and she was enviably pleasant-looking, slender and youthful. He was not as professional or as deft as Ah Fang when he went about his work, but was equally earnest and solicitous in dealing with people. That night he tried to persuade me to buy a bunch of bananas, half of which were hopelessly overripe and inedible. Not one to give up so easily, he followed me into the drizzle, saying repeatedly, when I was already dozens of paces away from the stand:

"If you don't have enough money with you, pay me some other day."

One day when I was buying some lychees, Ah Fang struck up a conversation with me:

"I see you pass through here all the time. You must live on this street. What's the house number?"

I told her I didn't live on the street. I only passed through this street on my way to work.

She said, "I thought so." She tied the lychees in a bunch. I saw brownish pregnancy-triggered splotchy spots on her face. Her lips appeared less rosy than before, yet her fingernails were painted a bright red, in jarring contrast to the gnarly knuckles. I found it tasteless but not particularly objectionable in her due to her innocence. I asked her:

"Who transports the fruits to the stand? It can't be you, can it?"

She said, "My man does it. He goes to the Shilipu wharf either before or after work."

"But you own the license?" I asked.

"Yes, I am in between jobs." As she answered, the pregnancy spots on her face seemed to redden, and I didn't press her for more information.

With Ah Fang and her fruit stand, this street seemed much livelier, even when the sky was obscured by dark clouds.

It was late at night and a light rain was falling as I walked through the quiet street, now deserted, with all doors closed. From a distance I saw Ah Fang sitting with her prominent belly under a lamp, her head bowed over a sweater she was knitting. Not wishing to disturb her, I walked on the opposite side of the street. Her handsome profile slowly glided across my field of vision on the other side of a street whose pavement glistened with rain.

After a time the fruit stand folded, probably because Ah Fang had given birth. As a result the street became markedly more deserted and much quieter, rain or shine. Her door was closed. A closed door is like a drop of water converging into the sea, anonymously receding into the long row of almost identical doors. Now I could no longer figure out which one was Ah Fang's door. I should have made a mental note of the number over the door when the stand was still open for business. But Ah Fang was so insignificant in this wide, vast world. After a while, I got used to a street that no longer had a fruit stand, my memory of it having faded with time. As far as I was concerned, this street was merely a road of passage on which I shuttled between home and work, the parts of my life that truly counted. As far as this street was concerned, I was but a transient, a traveler having nothing to do with the lives behind those identical doors.

I continued my daily passages through this by now familiar street paved with concrete slabs. Even ice cold droplets of water dripping down from the clothes strung on green-skinned bamboo poles sticking out of the street-facing windows seemed well acquainted with me and often landed naughtily on my forehead. Sometimes colorful soap bubbles parachuted from above and I would collect one in the middle of my palm, like a dream illuminating me. To me, it was a child's dream, bursting silently, leaving a wet, slippery trace on my palm, only to be followed by another, even prettier one that drifted down, and chased after me. In winter and in summer, in autumn and in spring, through cloudy days and shiny days, the street and I became so familiar with each other that there was no novelty, surprise or excitement left between us. Except for this once. It was a clear, crisp morning after a force 10 typhoon. A purple rose that had broken off from its branch suddenly fell from the second level

of a building facing the street to land on my
shoulder and subsequently by my feet. As
if on cue I thought of Ah Fang. She must
be a mother now, I thought. Was it a boy or
a girl? She probably was not going back to
selling fruits any time soon.

But Ah Fang was back selling her fruits.
One unremarkable late evening after many
unremarkable days, Ah Fang resurfaced,
with the same bangs cascading over her
eyes, the same bright eyes, the same pullover
emblazoned with red flowers and the same
fair complexion, quietly tending the same
fruit stand with a variegated display of
colors. The difference was a plump, fair-
skinned baby with the same rosy, supple lips
in her arms. The slender Ah Fang holding a
plump baby was an endearing picture. She
didn't seem to recognize me as she said in
her standard, friendly voice:

"Can I sell you something?"

I picked a bunch of bananas, which she
weighed after putting the baby in a baby
carriage in front of the door. I saw on her

third finger a thick gold ring that gave off a dull sheen.

Once again the neighborhood had a fruit stand, and with it, Ah Fang, her man and her baby. Ah Fang became acquainted with me as time went on, or more accurately she remembered who I was. Every time I passed by, she would call out to me, inviting me to buy something or asking whether the fruits I bought the previous day were sweet. I was afforded the privilege of buying on credit at the stand, although I never exercised that privilege.

The baby boy grew imperceptibly and Ah Fang grew fatter without appearing so. She maintained a slender figure and her handsome features. A hefty gold chain appeared on her neck as well a few delicate bracelets on her wrist. At night, under a lamp connected via a long cord to the house current, Ah Fang knitted her sweater, her man read and the baby boy learned to walk inside a baby walker. The fruits on the stand varied seasonally. Not infrequently a few rare, and therefore expensive, fruits, such as mangos, lay regally among the more numerous and more mundane fruits.

This picture of simplicity and harmony often moved me. It conveyed a down-to-earth strength and outlook on life and seemed to reveal the primitive origin and essence of life. On days filled with boredom and anxiety, the sight of Ah Fang, or even of that dim light outside Ah Fang's door, had a calming effect.

One night, it rained cats and dogs, the raindrops exploding into tiny watery pearls as they hit the ground with a splash. The street was nearly deserted by pedestrians; bicycles swooshed by and disappeared in a flash. As I walked by, I saw that business was slack in front of Ah Fang's house. A light shone through the open door. All of a sudden I heard a voice call out to me. Muffled by the rain it appeared to come from far away. I turned my head toward the sound and found it was Ah Fang's husband at the door. He said that the day's

muskmelons were excellent. If they turned
out not to be as sweet as promised, I needn't
pay. Or I could buy now and pay later. With
a smile, I folded my umbrella and walked
in. The baby boy was asleep, covered by a
pink terrycloth blanket, a finger stuck in
his mouth. Ah Fang was watching a live
broadcast of a Shanghai opera competition
on a 20 inch TV. Inside the house I saw a
refrigerator, a twin-tub washing machine,
a ceiling fan and a cassette player/recorder.
I picked some muskmelons from the crate
and paid for them. Ah Fang's man invited
me to sit for a while to wait out the pouring
rain.

It was indeed pouring. I did not leave
immediately but did not sit down either. I
chatted with him on my feet. I asked:

"Just the three of you live here?"

He said yes, the mother died the year
before; she had lived in the loft.

Only then did I notice the loft, which
was half the width of the room. Its wooden
sliding door meticulously painted a creamy

yellow was kept discreetly closed.

"Do you make a good profit selling fruit?" I asked.

"It depends," he said. "Like last summer, there was an oversupply of watermelons and, with the unseasonably cool temperatures, the price of watermelons fell sharply. As a result we lost hundreds of yuan. The loss was even greater in state-run stores." He laughed, as if the thought provided some solace. Although he was heavily built, I found in his features and facial expressions a trace of the educated man. I asked him what he did for a living. He said he was only a factory worker and was able to come up from the countryside where he had been resettled in the Cultural Revolution because his mother's death had enabled him to take over her city residence permit.

A thought flashed through my mind. I recalled that many years before I had passed by this spot and had seen a dilapidated, decaying interior through an open door. There was a son, and a mother. Probably it was here, yes, it must be here. I became agitated. Ah Fang was singing along with the contestants on TV. She was so absorbed in singing the arias of "Baoyu Crying over Daiyu's Death" (a story in *A Dream of Red Mansions*) she was totally unaware of the intrusion of the stranger that I was. Looking at her, I thought, could she be the one who had salvaged a family on the brink of collapse, brought relief to the impoverished life of a mother and a son and extended their lives and glories?

But I wasn't sure if this was the spot where I had seen that decaying home. All the doors looked so much alike, indistinguishable once closed. I was at once eager and afraid to have it corroborated. I was afraid of the disappointment of a guess proved wrong, of a dream shattered. I willed that this was that home I'd seen before. It was my pious hope. I decided to leave immediately. The rain had become heavier in the meantime, prompting Ah Fang's man to insist that I stayed. Even Ah Fang turned her head to say, "Stay a while longer."

But I left despite their insistence.

I practically fled from Ah Fang's home, finding my way by the weak illumination from the light inside the house, never once looking back. I was afraid that I would be tempted to inquire, to verify, and that would be so superfluous and silly. I didn't want the beautifully constructed story to collapse like a house of cards. I wanted it to stand, to stay with me.

Thus I've woven a beautiful fairytale of my own, to serve as a salutary reminder, when the mood or the weather is gloomy, to never lose heart. And I have carefully written down this fairytale in the hope that it will become an anonymous legend of this anonymous little street, to accompany Ah Fang's baby boy as he grows up and to last until the end of time.

The Grand Student

He was known among folks from Xibei village as Daxuesheng ("college student" or "grand student".) In their dialect *xue* is pronounced *xia* ("blind") with a short vowel, giving it a disparaging tone.

As the lunar New Year's Day approached, the migrant workers from Xibei village working on a job in the Liangcheng Apartments, in the northeast corner of the city, were giving the final touches to the apartment. As the end drew near, these migrant workers vacillated between going home to their village to reunite with family and looking for work that would stretch into the following year to augment their income so that they could afford to send for their wife and children to enjoy a very special New Year's Day in the big city. As a result of their wavering, the little work that remained to be done in the Liangcheng Apartments dragged on. The owner of the apartment, who came every day to inspect work progress, was becoming impatient and had increasingly harsher words for the workers, who simply wouldn't be hurried. When work was finally completed and the apartment was ready for the owner's inspection and acceptance, a gap was found in the paneling on one wall, and it had to be corrected. They were anxious to get paid so that they could think about what to do next. The uncertainties had led to unsteadiness in their worked and they seemed to have lost their surefootedness. It was at this juncture that the Daxiasheng came into their midst at the Liangcheng Apartments.

Xibei village has a tradition of producing

carpenters. Having learned carpentry skills under the tutelag of the masters, the apprentices would then come to this city to seek work. With their hard-earned money, they had been able to build three-story houses for themselves back in their village. All wood-related work in these houses, both in construction and in interior furnishing, was done by them with meticulous care. They never used nails but only mortise-and-tendon joinery. In the city, however, they worked differently: They used nail guns, like modern construction workers. With the air compressor plugged in, they would pop nails as if wielding a machine gun. In the city, premium is put on efficiency, so they obliged by being efficient. They were all smart, resourceful younger-generation carpenters, who had solid skills passed down from their masters, but had a broader perspective than their mentors and were good at embracing innovation. Because of this open-mindedness they remained much in demand in this city. This Liangcheng

Apartments job employed only a handful of
the Xibei migrants in the city. Many others
were scattered throughout the city working
in different new developments. Daxiasheng,
who was from Liyu hamlet of Xibei village,
had a cousin called Li Wen'ge working on
the job in the Liangcheng Apartments. Li
had worked in the city for three years now,
and Daxiasheng came looking for him upon
his arrival in the city.

But Daxiasheng didn't find Li Wen'ge
there. It so happened that Li, along with
Xue Hongbing, younger brother of his wife,
had left to work on a job downtown. Xue
Hongbing had arrived earlier that year
with no prior carpentry training to do
miscellaneous work under Li Wen'ge. The
Xibei folks told Daxiasheng that Li Wen'ge
had found work downtown just the day
before through Lao Gu, a plumber who
had worked with him before. Li Wen'ge
had therefore decided to stay in the city for
New Year's Day. When Daxiasheng asked
for the address of the job downtown, no

one knew; but they all thought he would be back one of these days to settle with the apartment owner and get his pay. That night Daxiasheng shared the bed of one of the Xibei workers. He also shared his food. He did not come from their hamlet but they knew each other and were kin because they were all related, be it remotely, in some way. But the Xibei workers were not particularly chummy with Daxiasheng, talking to him as little as possible and keeping him at arm's length, as if afraid he'd glom onto them.

He was nicknamed Daxuesheng, because he was a student. He was indeed a student as the sobriquet indicated, but he was no college student. The character "*da*" ("big or grand") was used figuratively to denote his grand style. Of course it also connoted his none too small age. Daxuesheng was actually a high school student who had graduated years earlier and was now over 30 years of age. His child was only three years old because he married late. He did not get into college after graduating high

school. He didn't want to learn a trade. As
for farming, he thought it way beneath his
dignity. Besides, there wasn't much land to
farm. Between his parents, his brothers, and
later his wife, the land was tilled and planted
in no time at all. He was rarely home year in
year out. He was always traveling. On rare
sightings, he would always be seen hurrying
somewhere, a brightly colored nylon bag
slung over his shoulder, either embarking
on a trip or just returned from a trip. In the
beginning his family still pinned their hopes
on him but eventually they gave up. Nobody
knew what he was up to. If you asked, his
reply was always incomprehensible and
he acted as if he was "playing the harp to
a cow" implying he was wasting his time
trying to explain an abstruse matter to a
fool. He left an impression that he was in
some mysterious business. But by and by
word came back from people who'd left
their native village to work in cities that
Daxiasheng was all the while cadging food
and drink from them and even got himself

a wife while so doing.

The girl he eventually married was from Anhui Province and had been helping at a home furnishing store run by her elder sister and brother-in-law, babysitting their child, and cooking for them. When Daxiasheng joined his fellow village folks here, the latter had been working in the alley where this furnishing store was located and had been buying most of their supplies—locks, wall outlets, hinges, nails and treads in the store, which were delivered by the girl. That was how she met Daxiasheng and began dating him. Undoubtedly she felt lonely and unappreciated helping in her sister and brother-in-law's store and was particularly eager to extricate herself from the setup and have a family of her own. Another factor might be that historically people from Anhui have aspired to life in wealthy Jiangsu Province, even in its less wealthy north. Or maybe it was the education Daxiasheng had had that attracted her to him. Anyway she cast her lot with the much older Daxiasheng without the least hesitation and settled with him in his native village. But Daxiasheng did not settle down to a sedentary, married life. Soon he resumed his traveling.

It was in the guise of a visiting relative that Daxiasheng called on the village folks who furnished new apartments for a living. He was neatly dressed in a pair of well-ironed dark slacks, a colorful, fashionable cowboy-style shirt and wore polished but conservative-looking black cowhide cap toe shoes. His hair was slickly parted at the side and the facial cream he applied on his face gave off a feminine odor. Slung on his shoulder was a colorful satchel normally seen on the backs of students taking holiday trips. Outwardly he combined the features of a city slicker and a country bumpkin, of tradition and modernity. In any case, his appearance at a work site where men from his village toiled in a haze of whirling sawdust was a visual clash and he looked out of place. He didn't seem to mind and squatted unobtrusively in a corner, watching their busy activity, asking them about pay and generally showing interest in and sympathy for problems in their lives. If the owner of the apartment made his appearance, he would walk up to him and shake his hands enthusiastically, passing a cigarette to him and bringing up the weather and current events as if he were a friend of his. When the owner made suggestions and demands in the course of inspecting work progress, he would instantly assume the role of a spokesman for the migrant workers, haggling and reasoning with the owner. The problem was he was not personally involved in the work, and was therefore not only clueless about what was going on but also did not possess the requisite technical savvy. As a result all he was capable of was mouthing disjointed, inane and useless generalities. A tough owner would shove him to one side, telling him to stay out of it, and pursue the matter with whoever was directly involved. Rebuffed so cavalierly, Daxiasheng would feel embarrassed and deeply offended. He would not openly incite his village folks to rebellion but would privately urge them to stage a walkout. But the workers from his village had come all the way to the city to work and they found it only natural that they should hear criticisms from the owner. They were afraid that his meddling would hurt their business; on the other hand they did not want to cause him to lose face by outright refusal of his intervention, which would give the impression that they did not appreciate his help or did not stand united with one of their own. So they went along, just to humor him, but inwardly they prayed that he would move along as soon as possible. Occasionally a congenial, generous owner would take the crew to a small food stall nearby at mealtime where he would order food and beer as a reward for the crew's hard work. On such occasions, Daxiasheng would be filled with anxiety and tense anticipation, worried by the prospect of not being included among the invitees to a supper he very much looked forward to. When he was finally seated at the table and his mind was set at ease, he would hold forth on different subjects, taking center stage, clinking glasses with the owner and bombarding the company with pedantic, high-flown rhetoric about some lofty theme or other. But the owner, obviously supremely indifferent to his overtures, would drink up his beer and tell the restaurant owner to bring the food to the table for the guests, and then signal that the feast was over. Daxiasheng had counted on a good chat with the apartment owner, whose premature departure would leave him silent and wistful.

Daxiasheng moved from one work site with Xibei migrant workers to another, always managing to find someone who would take him in, although without much enthusiasm. The way he dressed and the airs he put on led people to believe that he would find odd jobs beneath his dignity, so they refrained from offering any to him and treated him as a guest. As he passed through the various work sites, he made some discoveries. He discovered the exploitation of the migrant workers by the contractors. To his mind, the contractors gained without pain. They just happened to find themselves in an advantageous position between an apartment owner who needed to have his new, bare apartment furnished and readied for occupancy and the army of migrants desperate for work. He profited by acting as a sort of matchmaker. He wondered why the migrants themselves couldn't find the apartment owners looking to furnish and finish their newly acquired, but not yet partitioned or furnished apartment without going through an intermediary. By eliminating the extra expenditure of the contractor, the apartment owners could cut costs and the migrants stood to benefit from higher pay. Wouldn't that be a win-win situation for both? At bedtime, when the villagers started trashing the contractors for their shabby treatment of the workers, he would seize on the opportunity to expound his theory to them, but the migrants started snoring before he had a chance to finish.

This time around Daxiasheng came to the Liangcheng Apartments ostensibly to pay a visit to his cousin Li Wen'ge. Having been told that Li would be back one of these days to collect his wages, he settled down to wait for his return. As mentioned above, the workers' minds were elsewhere with New Year's Day approaching and work on the apartment drawing to an end. Most of the migrants had gone out during the day to find new work or to buy provisions to take back to the village for the New Year's Day celebrations. They would straggle back in the evening to continue putting quick finishing touches to the project before hitting the sack. Daxiasheng would pace or read in the bare room reeking of saw dust, glue and the body odors absorbed by the quilts. When it was time for lunch at midday, he decided to forgo the meal

because he couldn't cook with others' rice
or flour without permission and he was
not going to make do with the cold rice left
over from the previous day. At about three
in the afternoon a key turned in the lock.
The person who walked in looked at him
in surprise and asked, "Where are they?"
Guessing that this must be the owner of
the apartment, he walked up to him and
said that the guys were out running some
errands and would be back soon and that
he could pass on any messages. The person
asked, "Who are you?" "A friend dropping
by," he answered. Ignoring him, the owner
walked through the various rooms of the
apartment, inspecting the work in obvious
impatience and anger. Following him
about on his inspection tour of the house,
Daxiasheng asked about his profession and
whether the unit had been purchased by
him or was part of his employment benefits.
He proffered a cigarette to the owner as he
talked. The owner made no replies as if
he hadn't heard a word and snubbed the

cigarette offer. Talking to himself, he found fault with numerous aspects of the work. After the walkthrough the owner made straight for the door, turning a deaf ear to Daxiasheng's attempted explanation. At the door, the owner paused to take a good look at him and demanded to see his ID card. Daxiasheng's first reaction was to resist, but he suppressed his pride and produced the card. The owner, whose gesture was meant to signal his distrust, didn't really examine the card; he handed it back after a cursory glance. Then he left and slammed the door shut.

Daxiasheng, once again left alone in the house, was gnawed by hunger pangs and rankled by the cold-shoulder treatment he'd just received. Out of self spite, he went into the kitchen, added boiling water to leftover rice, opened a small pack of preserved vegetable and made quick work of the ersatz lunch before lying down on someone's bedding to read. He became groggy after a while but when he laid aside the book sleep

wouldn't come. The skull-piercing sound
of an electric drill being used in another
apartment shattered the quiet. He didn't
find the noise objectionable; on the contrary
it was a kind of antidote to his loneliness.
The light was fading now and the grayish
cement façade of the apartment building he
could see from the window dampened his
spirits and left him feeling sad. He began
to wonder if his cousin Li Wen'ge would
make it back that evening. His reverie
was interrupted by the sound of someone
coming in through the door. It was one of
his fellow villagers. His spirits lifted, he got
up to tell the new arrival that the owner had
come by and left after chatting with him
for a while. The worker from his village
mumbled an acknowledgment before going
into another room to put up wallpaper
around the door. The man was formally
dressed for his errands in the city: a suit
over a woolen sweater, brown leather shoes
polished to a fashionable muted shine. For
a minor job like this he didn't change into

his work clothes and the shiny new shoes on the work ladder gleamed softly and proudly before the eyes of Daxiasheng. The sight was a little too much for the latter to bear and he withdrew to his spot by the door. He was on the point of lying back down when a knock was heard on the door. To his surprised joy, it was his cousin Li Wen'ge at the door with his brother-in-law Xue Hongbing.

Li Wen'ge didn't seem particularly pleased to see his cousin and entered the apartment with his head bowed, making straight for the kitchen to put on the electric kettle. The brother-in-law, evidently in a foul mood, went to the bathroom to relieve himself. The two appeared to have suffered some major setback and were very reluctant to talk about their recent experience. They merely asked the guy who had come back ahead of them whether their wages had been settled. Daxiasheng discovered to his disappointment that, once again, he couldn't put a word in edgewise in this conversation and was reduced to standing there the odd man out. Soon however with the return of the rest of the crew, who immediately started hammering away and shooting nails with the nail gun under the full glare of several 200-lumen light bulbs, all geared up for a night of hard work, Li Wen'ge seemed to forget the unpleasant memories of recent days and cheered up considerably. He glazed the lattice glass door with practiced ease. The glass panes were poorly cut, with irregular edges and off-specs measurements, but he was still able to snugly fit them in before nailing in the wood trims that kept the panes in place. The result was quite professional-looking and he felt pride and satisfaction at the deft and effective control his hands exercised over the tools. Xue Hongbing in the meantime was already fast asleep and snoring loudly. He had just started learning the trade; well, it was not so much learning the trade as getting some experience working away from home. This kind of work and life offered little pleasure but a great deal of deep frustration.

The activity went on until about 8 p.m. when they put down their tools and started cooking rice, going out to buy beer and takeout food, which they set out on a door laid flat on some supports. The workers gathered around the makeshift table to eat their supper. After a few draughts of beer, Li Wen'ge, with a flushed face and bulging veins, launched into an account of the injustices and wrongs they had suffered in recent days. He told a halting story because he was not an articulate person to begin with and the emotion occasioned by his bitter experience didn't help smooth the flow of the story. So only a sketchy picture emerged from his account: They went to this job in a high-rise building, where the foreman was the plumber Lao Gu, who assigned them to work on installing the latticework underpinning wood floors. The lumber pieces, cut 2.8 meters long, couldn't make it into the elevator but Lao Gu would not allow them to cut them short to fit in the elevator and insisted that they be carried up 12 flights of stairs. When they drilled into the hard concrete floor, the drill bits quickly broke and they were told to replace them out of their own pocket. It had been agreed beforehand that the cost of transporting their heavy power tools to the work site would be reimbursed but they were refused reimbursement because they had transported the machinery in a taxi instead of a motorbike for disabled persons as instructed. This was the gist of the story distilled from a jumble of words. Xue Hongbing drank his beer in silence, touching neither the takeout food nor the rice, and refused to answer any questions. It fell to Li Wen'ge to recount the shabby treatment Xue had received: When they reasoned with Lao Gu, the latter rudely and violently shoved Xue to one side, saying, "I am not talking to you. You are only a helper."

After hearing him out, some joined the chorus of criticism against Lao Gu to make them feel better, while others tried to mollify them by explaining that Lao Gu was harsh with words but kind at heart, that he was a decent man. Didn't he treat everybody to a bowl of noodles with mutton last time they worked on the same job? He was not cunning like most of the locals and surely wouldn't treat them badly. They might as well try out the job and get paid after the flooring job was done. If the pay was good, they could stay, otherwise they could say goodbye to Lao Gu and split. Li Wen'ge responded by saying, "That's what got my goat! Lao Gu said we were to do the floors and nothing else. You know that after the floor supports are nailed down and the cement is poured, we'd have to wait at least ten days for the cement to dry before we can lay the wood floor. What are we to do during the ten days? We would be idle." If this was true then they believed Lao Gu was to blame. But they reckoned that having been in this business for some time and now himself a building contractor Lao Gu should know the work sequence of carpenters: When waiting for the cement to dry, they normally would hang cabinets or install door frames before laying the floor, to avoid idling the workers. They wondered if it was Li Wen'ge who misunderstood Lao Gu or Lao Gu who was not being reasonable. Getting nowhere in their attempt to mollify the aggrieved, they changed the subject and the matter was dropped.

A worrywart who had a tendency to excessively brood about costs and benefits and who was introverted to boot, Li Wen'ge had a hard time working a grievance out of his system and obsessed about it. He tossed and turned in bed, unable to calm himself down. Daxiasheng offered to go and reason with Lao Gu the following day but Li Wen'ge said he was not convinced of his cousin's ability to change Lao Gu's mind. To this Daxiasheng replied, "If he can't be brought to reason, you'll simply quit." There's plenty of work with so much new construction going on across the city. Li Wen'ge countered that on the other hand there were armies of migrants looking for work. At least this job would seamlessly dovetail with his current employment so that he wouldn't have to lose a single day of work. If he were to quit the new job, he'd have to wait past the New Year's holidays before he could find something else. That would mean a dozen days worth of lost income. Once the New Year's holidays were over, there would be a surge of migrants seeking employment and he might not be able to find a job for a fortnight or a month. That would be disastrous because he had not yet saved enough to buy all the materials he needed for building a new home back in his village. Besides, he had to support his sick parents at home and younger sisters still in school. The more he thought about it the less appealing the alternative appeared. The livelihood, the survival of his family literally depended on this new job! So maybe he should just grin and bear it. But how could he bear it? Lao Gu already said he was hiring them only for the floor job.

After the cement was applied, it couldn't possibly cure in three days, even five days. What was he to do during those days? Just sit there dipping into his savings? Then in another ten days, a fortnight or maybe twenty days—it looked like snow was on the way—how much would he earn for the floor job? The local carpenters shunned floor jobs precisely because they were the lowest paying and most back-breaking kind of carpentry work. Li Wen'ge was pulled in different directions by too many considerations: He couldn't afford to do it; no, he couldn't afford not to do it.

After giving the matter some thought, Daxiasheng seemed to hit on an idea. He asked his younger cousin whether he had met the owner of the apartment he would be working on. Li replied that they'd met a few times. Daxiasheng asked another question: what does he do? Li said he was probably a teacher of some sort because he had heard Lao Gu call him "Zhang Laoshi" ("Teacher Zhang"). Mr. Zhang the teacher was quite gracious and had agreed to pay for new drill bits to replace the broken ones. It was Lao Gu who stopped the owner and decreed that Li Wen'ge was to take full responsibility for the drill bits. He also refused to reimburse him for the cost of transporting his machinery in a taxi. When they asked the teacher-owner for cash to buy rice and other foodstuffs when Lao Gu wasn't around, Mr. Zhang gave them thirty yuan, to their pleasant surprise. So the owner was more congenial than Lao Gu. Daxiasheng asked, "Do you have the owner's beeper or phone number?" Despite his state of confusion, Li Wen'ge was alert enough to feel alarmed and asked him, "What do you want the numbers for?" He knew that this older cousin of his was a busybody capable of stirring up things which, more often than not, ended up badly for whoever he set out to help. Who knows what hare-brained ideas he's hatching in his head, he thought. Li Wen'ge felt he was already in deep enough trouble and didn't need his cousin's often counterproductive help. Warily he said he didn't remember the numbers and turned away feigning sleep to cut short the conversation. And the feigned sleep turned into an uninterrupted slumber from which he woke up only when it was light.

The following morning after finishing his breakfast in sulky silence Li Wen'ge started collecting his tools without looking up. Daxiasheng understood what he was up to and asked, So you still intend to go back to that job? Li Wen'ge did not answer but Xue Hongbing said, leaping up from his bedding, "You go alone! I'm not coming with you." Daxiasheng said with indignation, "Li Wen'ge! You are so spineless! Have you forgotten all the grievances you aired last night?" Faced with the stinging criticism from his two relatives, Li Wen'ge sat down helplessly. "What do you want me to do?" Xue Hongbing turned and left the apartment, slamming the door: I'm going to buy the bus ticket to go home for the Spring

Festival. He clambered down the stairs in furious, noisy strides until his footsteps could no longer be heard. Daxiasheng asked again, "Do you have the owner's beeper or phone number?" After a pause and some mental struggle Li Wen'ge took from a torn piece of paper from his pocket and handed it to Daxiasheng, who proceeded alone to the public phone stall outside the gate of the community and dialed the number.

The phone was picked up after one ring and a female voice came on the line. Daxiasheng asked, "Is this the Zhang residence?" The female voice said, "Yes. Who is this?" He said he was Li Wen'ge's elder brother. There was a pause at the other end of the line and he added, "I'm the elder brother of Li Wen'ge, the carpenter working on your apartment." "Oh, I see," said the female voice. "What's the call about?" He said, "I'd like to talk to you." The female voice retorted, "I don't even know you." This unexpected answer caught him off guard and it was followed by a second question: "Where is Li Wen'ge? Let me speak to him." He said, "Li Wen'ge is right here. He authorized me to talk to you on his behalf." The woman paused, apparently making an effort to keep her cool, and asked, "What does he want to talk about?" He feverishly collected his thoughts and blurted out the opening salvo of the script he'd been rehearsing all night: "Furnishing an apartment is a major, major event …" Before he could get to the next sentence, the woman cut him off with a laugh, "Not necessarily!" That left him speechless. In his flustered state he became a bit incoherent and reckless, raising his voice, "Lao Gu is not a trustworthy guy. You don't know him." The woman ignored him, saying "I don't know you, and hung up." He stood at the public phone counter, his heart beating wildly, staggered by the blow. It didn't occur to him that the woman truly did not know him and was already as civil as could be to have allowed the conversation to go on for as long as it did simply on account of his alleging to be Li Wen'ge's older brother. What more did he expect?

Li Wen'ge had at some point in time come down and quietly planted himself behind him, so when he turned he was startled by his presence. He asked, "What are you doing here?" Li Wen'ge said stutteringly, "I am going to the job. It's very far from here. It takes a few bus transfers and about two hours to get there." Daxiasheng's face darkened as he said in frustration, "Li Wen'ge! If I were Lao Gu, I would take advantage of you too." Li Wen'ge said defiantly, "I have to work. I left my wife and kids behind to come to this city for no other purpose than to work, didn't I?" It was a veiled jab at his older cousin, who had left his wife and family behind, but not for the purpose of finding work. Smarting from the hidden barb in Li's reply, Daxiasheng said with greater cruelty, "Has Lao Gu given you work? Besides the floor job, what else has he done for you?" Li Wen'ge, who had a mild temperament and was never good at

confrontation, didn't know what to say and
turned to leave. Instead of going out of the
community he went to sit on the concrete
wall of a raised flower bed. He appeared
to be sulking and crestfallen. After a while
Daxiasheng walked slowly over to him and
sat down on the wall, keeping a distance. He
said with a more conciliatory tone, "We have
to stand up for our rights, or else we'll never
get any respect." Li Wen'ge did not utter a
word and the two sat there in an awkward
silence, both avoiding any mention of the
phone call to the owner's home, as if it had
never happened. It was an overcast day and
even in the warmer southern winter the
wind was rather chilly. They did not have
their padded cotton coats on. Li Wen'ge
was dressed in a gray suit and Daxiasheng
in jeans, their faces grayish and lips bluish.
Both appeared to be hunched from the cold.
Li Wen'ge was in a quandary: To go or not
to go to the job, that was the conundrum. It
would be much less of a dilemma for anyone
else but the decision was particularly

painful for him. He was afraid to lose the job but on the other hand he was equally afraid of offending Daxiasheng. He figured he had already antagonized one relative— his brother-in-law Xue Hongbing, who bore a grudge against Li Wen'ge for having allowed Lao Gu to treat him so shabbily. He couldn't afford to alienate yet another relative. Otherwise he'd end up ostracized for breach of trust and bowing to injustices. What was important now was not so much to redress his grievances as to placate the others. He was bitter but, not being able to bring himself to blame others, he blamed himself.

After spending the whole morning wallowing in self-blame and self-pity, Li Wen'ge forwent his lunch, causing Daxiasheng to do likewise. Li Wen'ge's mood weighed on Daxiasheng, who felt an obligation to solve Li's problems. The thought perked him up, despite his empty stomach, because it gave him something to do. He said, I'll go with you. Li Wen'ge kept his silence, with a hangdog look for almost twenty minutes before finally getting to his feet and breaking his silence. "Let's go then." The two of them walked out of the project.

On the way, Daxiasheng said to Li Wen'ge, You don't know how to talk, so keep quiet and leave the talking to me. Further along the way he added, "You may be afraid to antagonize people but I'm not. So leave it to me." All the while Li Wen'ge kept his own counsel and kept his distance from Daxiasheng, as if reluctant to be in his company. When on the bus, he would gravitate toward the more crowded part of the vehicle, either consciously or subconsciously trying to shake off Daxiasheng, who would appear to be tailing him. Once or twice Li Wen'ge darted into a store, with Daxiasheng in hot pursuit, asking what he was buying; he answered, "nothing, just browsing." This chase scene lasted until about four in the afternoon when they finally arrived at their destination. The gloom in the sky deepened, threatening snow, but the little street where Li Wen'ge found new work bustled with activity. It was actually an alley lined with shops, most of which were purveyors of home furnishing and building materials run by people from Fujian province catering to the needs of several newly completed apartment buildings in the alley ready for interior partitioning and furnishing. There were also hair salons operated by people from Wenzhou and fast food restaurants run by folks from Zhejiang and Jiangsu provinces. You ran into people from all regions of the country, speaking their respective dialects. Enforcement of traffic rules was lax in the alley, which had turned into a two-way thoroughfare. As cars going in opposite directions met in the narrower parts, they had to maneuver left and right, honking their horns, to avoid scraping and scratching each other, turning the place into a veritable country fair. The neighborhood had more human and vehicle traffic than the area around the Liangcheng Apartments, but was also much noisier.

Passing through the bustling little street they came into the enclosed community where the new apartment was located. The building was a high-rise with a silver gray façade with a red trim going around its midriff. It had a more imposing look than the Liangcheng Apartments. The security guard on the ground floor recognized Li Wen'ge and let them through. The elevator, an automatic one made by Mitsubishi, rose quietly and stopped with a "ding" at the desired floor and quietly opened its door. There was the buzzing sound of a power drill somewhere in the building and hammering, but the place still had a cavernous feel to it. Li Wen'ge fished out a key and opened the door to the apartment, which had larger living and dining rooms and smaller bedrooms, unlike the units in the Liangcheng Apartments. In the middle of the living room a power saw was left lying on a thick coat of sawdust giving off a damp smell. Picking up thin wooden pegs from the floor and collecting them into a plastic bag, Li Wen'ge proceeded to the next room and started hammering the wooden pegs into predrilled holes in the cement floor. He wielded the mallet with forceful deftness and the pegs were soon knocked flush with the cement floor. Daxiasheng said, "Li Wen'ge! Why are you in such a hurry to get to work? Didn't we agree that we'd talk to the owner first before resuming work?" Li Wen'ge, deflated by the reproach, threw down the mallet and said, "There's no telling when he will show up." Daxiasheng said, "Call him on the phone now and ask them to come." He still didn't mention his call to the owner that morning and Li Wen'ge, as if by some tacit understanding, did not ask. Li Wen'ge reluctantly went out to make the call and Daxiasheng followed him, not trusting him to do it right. The two rode the elevator down in hostile silence.

Once out of the elevator, Li Wen'ge ran out of the community at a brisk pace. Not used to this kind of running, Daxiasheng soon lost sight of him. He decided to stay put and stood at the gate of the community waiting for his return. Opposite the enclosed community was a decommissioned factory being dismantled and moved to another location. It was now deserted and its high fence was topped with barbed wire which had snagged shreds of paper and broken plastic bags here and there. It was quite a forlorn sight. The wind was chillier now, the cold penetrating to the bone. Without the boost of the calories of lunch, which he had forgone, he found the cold even harder to bear. Not knowing how the day would end further saddened his heart. Then he saw Li Wen'ge walking toward him, accompanied by a man and a woman, apparently husband and wife, dressed warmly in ski sweaters, both tall and taking long strides, their eyes looking straight ahead. Li Wen'ge, thin and small in stature and dressed in flimsy clothes, was walking close to the wall, turning from time to time to speak to the couple, with a humble smile on his face. Daxiasheng couldn't help feeling disgusted by Li Wen'ge's timid, ingratiating attitude toward the couple.

Li Wen'ge hadn't made any phone calls but had been walking about in the busy, noisy alley, stalling for time and putting off the moment of confronting Daxiasheng. He had no idea what the outcome of the stalling would be. Then he ran into the owners when he least expected it. They asked him what he was doing there and he said he was going to call them. What was it about, they asked; he answered, he was running out of nails and he was going to ask them to buy some. The owner said, "Xiao Li, in minor matters such as nails, you can go right ahead and make the purchasing decision yourself." Improvising, Li Wen'ge said he was concerned that the owner might have already bought a new supply of nails and he didn't want to incur unnecessary expenses by buying more than was needed. The owner made nary a mention of the morning phone call by his "elder brother," for which Li Wen'ge was grateful. Gratitude turned into ingratiation and accommodation to everything the owner said. They arrived at the gated community while engaging in this kind of amicable exchange. Daxiasheng came out from behind the concrete pillar forming part of the gate to greet them, nodding to the couple, who ignored him. In the meantime Li Wen'ge had gone briskly ahead. Daxiasheng trailed behind the couple, introducing himself, "I am the elder brother of Li Wen'ge." But the couple did not slow down or deign to look at him. The woman said with a laugh, "So it was you who called this morning." At this, Li Wen'ge became apprehensive and further quickened his pace to run into the building. Daxiasheng was a little sheepish when confronted with this question; he asked evasively, "Where does Mr. Zhang work?" Without eliciting an answer from Mr. Zhang, he added, "We are working on an apartment in the Liangcheng Apartments. The owner works at East China

Technical University of Water Resources. He is an associate professor there." Mr. Zhang grunted an acknowledgment. "Is Mr. Zhang's apartment part of his employment benefits or has he bought it?" But Mr. Zhang had by now hopped on the steps and was exchanging greetings with the staff of the community's management office. After talking for a while, they took the elevator, with Daxiasheng following closely behind, to the 12th floor.

Li Wen'ge was already in the apartment and had turned on the electric kettle. He was sweeping the sawdust and putting it into a plastic woven bag. The predrilled holes in the cement floor came to the attention of Mr. Zhang the moment he entered his apartment. He took out a tape measure to measure the distances between holes. Apparently satisfied, he said to Li Wen'ge, getting up from his crouched position, "That will be the spacing for the screw holes for the floor support." Li Wen'ge responded by saying he would do one room first and

upon Mr. Zhang's inspection and approval
he'd go on to the other rooms. He spoke
as if nothing unpleasant had happened,
and all the bitterness he vented the night
before had been for naught. The couple left
instructions about minor details and both
sides exhibited substantial understanding
and agreement. Daxiasheng tried several
times to signal to Li Wen'ge with his eyes,
but the latter deliberately averted his eyes.
Unable to keep himself in check any further,
Daxiasheng finally spoke up. He said, "We'd
like to talk to you."

Mr. Zhang, who had made his way
toward the door, now paused and looked at
him in considerable surprise. The woman
wore an amused smile, her interest piqued.
Daxiasheng said, "Home furnishing is a
major event in life." Mr. Zhang cut him off
impatiently, "It's not major at all." He was
obviously eager to end this conversation.
Daxiasheng, his tactic once again frustrated,
became crimson in the face and emitted an
emotional cry, "You can't take advantage of

my younger brother like this." The woman, still smiling, asked Li Wen'ge, "Xiao Li, have we taken advantage of you?" Li Wen'ge, choosing not to answer the question, bent down to unplug the electric kettle because the water had boiled. Daxiasheng said, "My brother was so angry he couldn't sleep last night. He is a simple soul not skilled at expressing himself and you take advantage of him." The woman pressed Li Wen'ge, "Xiao Li, have we taken advantage of you?" Li Wen'ge blew air at the kettle to cool the water and drank from it but remained silent. Mr. Zhang was not so nice about it. He took a step toward Daxiasheng and demanded, "What do you mean?" Daxiasheng, stunned by this new aggressiveness, softened his tone. "We carpenters contract for all carpentry work, not just floor work." Mr. Zhang riposted, "Who says your brother does floor work only?" The woman said to her husband that they didn't need to talk to him since they didn't know him at all. This got Daxiasheng worried; nothing could be worse than their refusal to talk to him. He could see that the woman was a tougher customer than the man. He felt compelled to defend his position in a raised voice. "I am speaking on my brother's behalf." The woman asked Li Wen'ge, "Is that so? Xiao Li?" Mr. Zhang, with a single-track mind, repeated his question: "Who says Li Wen'ge does floor work only?" Afforded a dignified ladder to climb down, Daxiasheng seized it and said with a smile, "It seems there has been some misunderstanding. I've always advocated direct dialogue bypassing the intermediary of Lao Gu. We have not only carpenters on our team, but also masons, painters … you name it. We normally contract for the entire, complete home furnishing job." When he realized no one had interrupted him, he got excited and became more eloquent. "Why do we need Lao Gu? Why a third party?" The woman laughed again. "Since when has Lao Gu become a third party? You are the third party." This rendered him temporarily speechless. The woman turned and said to Li Wen'ge, "It was through Lao Gu that we hired you to do carpentry work. If not for Lao Gu, how could we have come to know about you?" A sheepish smile appeared on Li Wen'ge's face as he continued to drink from the kettle. Daxiasheng said, "Li Wen'ge, Don't remain silent. Say it. Didn't Lao Gu tell you to do the floor only and nothing else? He wanted you to pay for the broken drill bits and refused to reimburse you for the cost of transporting the machinery. Isn't that the case?" The woman said with a serious face to Li Wen'ge, "Xiao Li! You can quit if you are not pleased with the arrangement. If you truly want to work, then let's forget about what happened today and we won't say anything to Lao Gu." Having been put on the spot, Li Wen'ge mumbled while continuing to drink from his kettle, "I give up!" Daxiasheng, much annoyed, said, "Then I'm going to take this machine with me. It's mine. We need it for other jobs." Startled, Li Wen'ge looked up and cast a glance at Daxiasheng. Chilled by this glance, Daxiasheng said with gritted teeth, "Li Wen'ge! If you give up, then don't expect me to help you in the future." His patience wearing very thin now, Mr. Zhang said, "We will ask Lao Gu to come and talk to you." Daxiasheng said, "When will Lao Gu be here?" Mr. Zhang said, "How about tomorrow? You discuss it with Lao Gu. We won't be here." Daxiasheng was on the point of agreeing when he suddenly realized that they had come full circle: they set out to eliminate Lao Gu as the middleman but now ended up having to deal with Lao Gu after all. He protested loudly, "That was a big mess-up!" The woman retorted, "What do you know about mess-ups?" Not wanting to continue the argument, Mr. Zhang dragged his wife out of the apartment and closed the door behind them.

It was suddenly very quiet in the room. Through the sliding door of the balcony, one could see a forest of high-rise buildings

with interior lights already turned on. In
the distance on a street whose streetlamps
had been lit, the columns of headlights of
the cars traveling in opposite directions
flowed like a river of lights. At some point
in time the sound of power drills had died
down, accentuating the ambient quiet.
Under the illumination of the lights, the
walls were white as snow and the large room
appeared vaster than usual. Compared
with the cluttered dorm at the Liangcheng
Apartments, this room could claim a de
luxe rating. They laid out their blankets on
the floor. Xue Hongbing had not yet taken
away his bedding, so it served as a bed for
Daxiasheng. He took out a few books from
his satchel and placed them by his pillow for
his night reading. He had made a cosy bed
in a quiet, snug corner. Meantime Li Wen'ge
was cooking rice gruel on his hot plate. He
was a frugal man, unlike some migrants who
were more liberal in pampering themselves
with creature comforts. He associated every
penny with the toil he put himself through

and the suffering involved in leaving behind home and family, and with the new home waiting to be built back in the village and a happier future. He minced some salted vegetable and began supper with Daxiasheng. With the windows closed and the heat of cooking, the room was toasty enough. The condensation forming a mist on the window panes dissolved the lights outside into a dispersed, blurry pattern of illumination. The cosy atmosphere rubbed off on both of them and they started to chat in a relaxed, serene state of mind. This was the first time in the day that they could talk to each other without rancor or hostility. It was an auspicious start to the evening.

The peacefulness was disturbed by a "ding" of the elevator stopping at their floor, followed by footsteps coming out of it and heading their way. Then the key turned in the lock and the door was opened, letting in Mr. Zhang and Lao Gu. Both were very tall and Lao Gu was stocky as well. Sitting on low stools, Li Wen'ge and his cousin instantly felt a threatening presence. Lao Gu said to Li Wen'ge straight away, "Xiao Li, you humiliated me!" Li Wen'ge did not say a word, his head bowed. Daxiasheng got to his feet to offer a cigarette, but Lao Gu didn't even look at him as if he did not exist. Lao Gu was a veteran worker who had become a plumber since his retirement from an electric machinery factory, which he joined at 17 as an apprentice learning from a master worker. He later passed down his skills to his own apprentices. He treated the migrant workers the same way he did his apprentices. Of course he was not immune to some of the feelings of typical Shanghainese about out-of-towners. He was a paternalistic type who considered yelling the normal way to speak. But, as observed by Li Wen'ge's fellow Xibei villagers, Lao Gu might be mean in speech but not at heart.

Lao Gu continued, "You have to enjoy your work. If you feel so miserable on this job, you can leave after finishing your meal." Daxiasheng immediately said, "How much

are you going to pay for the two days' work?"
Ignoring the question, Lao Gu turned to
Mr. Zhang and said, "Zhang Laoshi, it will
be four days of wages, plus transportation
to the building. You owe them a total of 250
yuan." Mr. Zhang settled the bill right away.
Daxiasheng had obviously wanted to raise
a stink but his attempt fizzled because Lao
Gu was not the petty type. Besides, there
were rules for employers, contractors and
workers. Whoever broke the rules would
have a hard time finding a livelihood in
this trade. After a pause, Daxiasheng said
conciliatorily, "Can we leave tomorrow?"
His words were loaded with such abject
sadness and his tone was so beseeching that
even the weak-willed Li Wen'ge considered
it totally uncalled for. Li put down his
bowl and immediately started packing. Mr.
Zhang, in reply to the appeal of Daxiasheng,
said, "You might as well leave as soon as
possible. Didn't you say you needed the
machine for other jobs?" By now Li Wen'ge
had finished packing; he picked up his bag

and uttered the most candid and upbeat words ever to issue from his mouth, "Now I can go home for the Spring Festival!"

Finally the two of them carried the machine and their bags out of the apartment. Lao Gu and Mr. Zhang stayed behind and could be heard from the elevator to be hammering at the door lock. They were changing the lock. Although Li Wen'ge surrendered the key, he could no longer be trusted as a result of the bad blood.

The wind was chilly but fortunately they felt warm. Or maybe it was anger that insulated them against the cold. They walked across the apartment community still under construction, with no streetlamps, and piles of bricks and sand strewn about. It was inevitable that they tripped against these unseen obstacles. Even before they came out of the building site, they were already greeted by the noise coming from the street outside. There were two entirely different worlds. In the high-rise buildings of the community, it was quiet and comfortable, but here one entered the rough-and-tumble world. When they came out of the building site they saw three migrant workers lined up at the foot of the high wall across the street, facing the wall in a dubious posture. Then they realized the three were relieving themselves as they heard the sound of rushing water. The three were oblivious to the cars and passers-by at their backs, bantering among themselves as they answered the call of nature. When these people left their village and home to come to an unfamiliar city they also seemed to leave behind any sense of shame, decency or decorum. The lights in a few hair salons remained lit and girls working in them leaned against the door, eyeing the passers-by suggestively. The way they dressed and their accent still identified them as out-of-towners, but already some of the city ways and fashions had rubbed off on them, creating an impure mixture of clashing tastes. Further along, a tussle was going on in a dark corner, a soundless tableau of people tangling with and tearing at each other. Picking their way through the throng, they finally made it to the main road, where they waited for a taxi. The cars whooshed by and came to a simultaneous halt at the red light, their headlights burning indifferently. When the taxi they hailed approached and found them to be migrant workers, and carrying a heavy piece of machinery to boot, the driver refused to take them and drove away from the curb to merge into the moving traffic.

Their long exposure to the elements had by now dissipated the heat reserve in their bodies and they began to feel the cold. The traffic in the street slowed down a bit; finally a taxi flashing its right front light slowed down by the curb and stopped in front of them. The driver said nothing about their bags and the machine, apparently a good-natured driver eager for business. He came out to open the trunk for them to put their stuff in, but insisted on their sitting in the back seat. In this season of year-end holidays, taxi drivers were extra alert to the danger of nighttime robberies, which had become increasingly frequent. They were especially wary of migrant workers from out of town like them. Li Wen'ge got in first and was sliding across the seat to make room for Daxiasheng, when the latter stuck his head in to say he was visiting a friend and closed the taxi door. Before Li Wen'ge had time to say anything, the car drove off. He watched Daxiasheng cross the street, braving the moving traffic, his back finally disappearing on the far side. From this angle, he did look like a city resident, and an educated city person at that. Indeed, he couldn't tell the difference between him and the other city people.

Li Wen'ge and his fellow Xibei villagers stayed two more days in Shanghai. Through an intermediary, they got two days worth of odd jobs working for the housing administration, repairing windows and doors. Then came the final days of the lunar year. On the night before the eve of the Lunar New Year's Day, failing to get long-distance bus tickets, they had to take the train to Zhenjiang, from where they ferried across the river to catch a bus. It was not an express bus and it stopped to pick up and let off passengers at every stop. The bus trip took all night. The train was also crammed full, with many standing tickets issued so that the aisles and the toilets were all fully occupied. A fellow villager went to the diner car to buy food to go with the beer they brought on board to make the long night more bearable. It was a long while before he was able to fight his way back. He saw Daxiasheng in another car in the train. He didn't say hello and Daxiasheng also pretended not to have seen him. It appeared Daxiasheng was also heading home for New Year's Day.

Inhabitants of
a Vintage Era

Some things, which are actually quite recent, turn into sepia-toned old photographs before one realizes it. Take the example of the city's railed streetcars, which seemed to be still running only yesterday. You'd walk east on the street just outside the alley, turn into the next street and you'd hop on the trolley. The conductor donning a uniform cap would walk over, staggering between the two rows of wooden seats, to sell you the ticket for three fen (1 yuan = 100 fen). But today not a trace of the rails is visible

on the streets. In late 1970, when they returned to Shanghai from the rural areas in
Anhui province where they had been settled,
the city's educated youth found swarms of
pedicabs waiting at the exits of the station
soliciting business and many of them were
taken home in one of those trishaws. In
the blinking of an eye, these three-wheeled
contraptions have taken on the glow of the
last aristocrats, a dull, sepia, indoorsy glow.
There is the opposite phenomenon of something obviously from another era that turns
out to be quite recent, after a consultation
with the historical chronicles. The Western
suit and the *qipao* (or cheongsam) are cases
in point. They gradually disappeared from
the scene only in the early to mid-1960s but
they've left a light, indifferent imprint on
the popular imagination, as if they were
merely stage props. Some celebrities in the
performing arts, such as Zhou Xuan, our
contemporaries, are now browned photos
marred by mildew spots, their singing voices coming out of the phonograph distorted

and scratchy!

Memories, they say, with good reason, are fragile; they are so easily supplanted. When a new store opens around the corner, you suddenly have difficulty recalling what the previous store sign read. When a new building goes up, you completely forget what the old building looked like. And when the city opens up a new street, you don't remember which way the old street ran. On the other hand, memory can be very stubborn and persistent, breaking through the rubble of layer upon layer of deposits of the past, following you, lurking in an obscure corner of your field of vision, waiting for a ray of light to strike from an angle to re-emerge from obscurity. Then you realize that you've been staring at it for a long time and it has stared at you for an equally long time. In this silent, mutual gaze, a sympathy slowly rises, expands and fills the space between you and the memory with a vast fogginess, separating you from it. Nevertheless you and the memory remain visible to each other, your silhouettes not blurred by the fog. At such moments, memory is so limber and resilient, the warmth of its body against yours slightly moist and sticky, its breath not particularly fresh but rather stale, like the odor emanating from the mouth of someone who has just woken up from a night's sleep or the odor of overripe fruit. It is palpable to such a degree that it is almost intimate.

One can hardly say memory is faithful to reality. It only has the semblance of realism. It depicts the minute details that appear vividly before your eyes, but is helpless when it comes to the deeper causes, for instance. This is because it always seizes on the surface phenomena; it is susceptible to emotions and is closer to instinct. It does not contain reason and therefore lacks cognitive power. One can even say that it collects information somewhat mechanically and waits passively for the information to be screened and sifted through. Who does the sifting? Much like a heavenly body, it spins and rotates in its orbit, in a constantly changing relationship with the light-emitting stars around it. It is therefore hard to pinpoint a fixed angle at which light is going to strike it. When it strikes, it will appear to be a random event, but the random outcome comes at the end of a long trip after much spinning and rotating. So it appears that there might be some kind of a purpose and preplanning. A light increases in intensity in a dark corner of the field of vision. It comes from the direction of the footlights on the stage. Then a Fresnel spotlight comes on in the wings, followed by the lights illuminating the backdrop. The ceiling lights remain dark while the spectators' sections fade into a profound darkness that accentuates the brightness of the stage. Then there is a stirring, a timid stirring, setting off distinct echoes nonetheless, which bounce about, back and forth, beginning, like a snowball, with an insubstantial, loose consistency, to gather increasing mass and volume, finally coalescing into a focused sound.

Under the illumination of the footlights the actors entering the stage invariably wear shadows above their facial features, over their eyebrows, in the hollows of their eyes, and front center, triangular in shape, on the bridges of their noses, above their lips and in the shallow depressions of their chins. The glaring darkness of the shadows is only attenuated and relieved by the light projected from the spotlights in the wings. Playing a modulating role, the lights on the backdrop further dilute the low lighting angle effect of the footlights, but at the same time separate, isolate the players from the background so that they float like wafer-thin scraps of paper over the light on the backdrop. The expressions in the subjects' faces have been obscured; the shadows cast by the low angle lighting split and then splice back the faces, creating a uniform look, a stereotype, much like the faces of alien races with whom no communication is possible—dull, wooden and inscrutable.

On to the story. It was a hot, humid evening.
The moisture in the air had softened the
night to a lighter dark, without making
it any less opaque, the water molecules
blocking the passage of light, whose rays
seemed to have coagulated in place. The
night was accordingly of a thick consistency,
sweltering, not without a breeze, but a
breeze that, instead of blowing at you,
enveloped you like a palpable substance. It
was hot, but the heat brought out no sweat.
At certain spots in the street you might
even feel a chilliness that caused goose
bumps, although your pores remained
tightly closed. We were walking on a quiet
street, turning back when we reached the
end of the block and walking toward the
other end.

The section of Maoming Road closest to
Huaihai Road is situated in the west district
of the city. Walking north along Maoming
Road from the movie house at the corner of
Huaihai Road is a long gallery of expensive

stores, which were now dark. By the light
of the streetlamps, one could see displayed
in a window an exquisite chest ornament
made of felt and a rose-red broad-brimmed
hat, below which hung a pair of like-
colored slippers, a vivid, idyllic picture
of femininity with a hint of decadence. A
leather barber's chair reclined quietly, its
chrome parts gleaming demurely. Western-
style great coats hung unobtrusively in
the store. All the luxuriousness now lay
dormant, the flamboyance folded and
stored away for the moment. Behind the
gallery of luxury shops is the garden of
the venerable Jinjiang Hotel. If you walk
further down, you come to the corner of the
cross street Changle Road. Across the street
on Changle, at a corner, is the Shanghai
Art Theater, formerly the famed Lyceum
Theater. It was at this hour closed and a
streetlamp illuminated the tiled floor in
front of it. We came to a halt, considering it
reckless to cross Changle Road at this spot,
and walked instead further down Maoming

Road. As we looked about, we found only a handful of pedestrians, weaving in and out of the rows of Chinese parasol trees lining the street. Looking behind us, we found mother and her lady colleague, about 200 meters back, in the gallery of shops, still talking in hushed tones, without any sign of wishing us to join them. Apparently they needed more time for their confidences.

We searched with our eyes and found, across the street, on the west side of Maoming Road, a lone store that remained open, its florescent lights blazing, plunging the street outside the store into deeper darkness. Its big freezer facing the door was visible from the street, from where one could almost hear the humming of its compressor, and some human voices. There was life in there! My hand in my elder sister's hand, we looked cautiously right and left for passing cars. There were not many of them at that hour, but the occasional one would drive by at breakneck speed. If we couldn't dodge it fast enough, we ran the risk of being hit.

Finally, making sure it was all clear, we dashed across the street like two frightened rabbits, leaving behind the gallery of shops, the Jinjiang Hotel and the Shanghai Art Theater on the other shore. We paused for a few moments before the store, an average-sized confectionery selling candies, pastry and cold beverages. A cloying sweet smell of popsicles blew from the thickly frosted freezer. Two sales clerks were talking, their voices reverberating loudly. The florescent fixtures shone brightly on the interior, laying bare all the minute rundown and tired details. It had a stale look, so we turned and left after some hesitation. This side of the street is mostly residential, the windows overlooking the street now dark behind curtains or blinds. There was not a sound, although the night was still young, with time before the fourth showing at the movie house.

Mother had brought us for the fourth showing of the movie *Jie Zhenguo*, an adapted modern Beijing opera, in that movie house at the corner of Huaihai Road. A heavily made-up male in an operatic freeze-pose, the sleeve of his indigo blue shirt turned up to show the white lining, was depicted in a giant poster at the entrance to the cinema. Both the title of the film and its male actor looked disappointing, especially at such an hour. Our interest flagged even before the show started. We had, by design, been brought out well ahead of show time. Mother met up with her lady colleague and sent us on a stroll along the street ahead of them. When we turned our head occasionally to check on them, we would find them whispering into each other's ears in hushed tones, sometimes pausing as if a suspenseful moment had been reached in their confidences, bringing them to an involuntary halt. But soon they remembered they were walking in the street and quickly moved on, apparently not wishing people to know that they were engaged in a serious conversation. This heightened the sense that they must be discussing something they wanted to keep secret. They would disappear and reemerge from behind the rows of Chinese parasol trees. They were dressed for summer in light-colored, billowing one-piece dresses, flaring out from the waist. Their permed bobbed hair had been tied up with handkerchiefs because of the hot weather. We were in the early 1960s, when people of the city had not yet been discouraged from the pursuit of fashion and modernity, which even infected mother and her lady colleague, both of whom had been liberation fighters in the guerrilla bases before coming to the city!

We finally got fed up with shuttling back and forth along the same city block and decided to join mother and her colleague. Mother was startled when we appeared without warning at her side. She immediately took out some change from her purse and told us to get some ice cream for ourselves. So we were sent away again into the warm, humid night, leaving them alone, two diminutive figures among the dark looming parasol trees that appeared so gigantic to us. We started to feel a certain unease. The secretive talk between mother and her colleague, our solitary pacing back and forth on this quiet, deserted street and the dreary florescent light of the lone store still open for business combined to deepen the mystery of the night.

We marched toward the store, at a pace quickened by fresh purpose, although with no great joy in our heart. We were soon back in that store, which appeared more forlorn than before, the voices of the sales clerks bouncing off its four walls desultorily. We handed over our change and the man went to the freezer and lifted its lid. A blast of frigid air accompanied by a puff of white fog, blew into our faces, sending a chill through our bodies and making us feel sticky with the condensation of the moisture. As we peeled off the wrappings from the popsicles our fingers got all sticky from the softening ice cream. We were supposed to enjoy the ice cream despite this unclean feeling. Sucking at the tip of the popsicle, we turned around and walked back in the opposite direction. The popsicles turned into a thick, sweet liquid in our mouths, traveling toward our throats and then swallowed, the thrill in the split second of swallowing the sweet syrup inducing more gluttonous sucking. The ice cream melted quickly in the warm air and soon the sucking could no longer catch up with the melting. As a result the ice cream trickled slowly down our wrists and arms. All this was depressing and joy killing. Then we spotted the man and the woman.

We no longer have any memory of the dress the man was wearing, but the woman had on a *qipao* (also known as cheongsam). She was obviously old-school, wearing a *qipao* and high-heels, her hair permed, but not in the same style as mother's. She had long permanent waves, which fell somewhat untidily over her shoulders, for lack of combing. She did not have a handbag with her, as if she had left her home in a hurry. Oh yes, she did not wear

any makeup either. Normally women whose
hair was permed with long waves and wore
a cheongsam would apply makeup before
going out. In that era it was still possible
to see a few women dressed like that in the
streets of Shanghai. They radiated a tacky
elegance dressed in the fashion of a vintage
era, a gone-by dynasty. This tackiness smelt
of datedness and decline. They attracted
looks, not looks of envy or admiration, but
of surprise. She had a haggard look, but
who knows? On such an evening anybody
would have a haggard look. She and the man
walked side by side, an arm's length apart,
taking the same path as we did. The lateral
separation between them was subtle—not
too intimate and not too distant; they were
definitely not casual acquaintances. Even
the silence between them was unusual.
Unlike us, who walked at a leisurely, bored
pace, they walked briskly as if they had
a place to go to. So they overtook us and
for a while it looked like we were tailing
them and they stayed in our sight for

quite some time. The man was observed to surreptitiously edge closer toward the woman, who imperceptibly inched away, causing their path to gradually stray from the sidewalk into the street.

Then they dropped out of our sight, leaving unease in the air. It had already been an unsettling night, now they had heightened the suspense. We now approached the corner of Huaihai Road, but mother still did not signal us to join them. They must have reached a climactic point in their secret talk. We contemplated the poster at the entrance of the movie house. The image of the main character Jie Zhenguo occupied almost its entire surface, wearing a contemporary outfit but striking a traditional operatic pose with his fist resting in front of his chest at the end of an arc described by his out swinging arm. This was a movie with a contemporary theme but in the format of traditional opera, a genre that held no interest whatsoever for us. There were only a handful of people in

front of the cinema and on Huaihai Road.
Not much life was left in the city at that
hour. After the ice cream, which had left
sticky trails along our throats and arms, we
felt thirsty, but did not feel like drinking.
It was not a pleasant feeling. What to do?
We decided to turn back and continue our
perpetual motion. We found to our surprise
we were walking in the wake of the couple
once again. So they must have been going
back and forth in the neighborhood. While
we walked aimlessly, they definitely had a
problem to solve. We quickened our pace
to catch up. For a while we were abreast of
them. The streetlamps were blocked by the
dense foliage of the parasol trees and we
had to look at them out of the corner of our
eyes, because we couldn't very well turn and
stare at them. They still didn't speak to each
other. We saw the man raise his hand and
flick it at the woman's face, as if to touch
it, or to slap her. Again the woman drew
back. These movements did not interfere
with their walk, which was maintained at

the same speed and rhythm. So we had to suspect that what we had just witnessed was an illusion. Something had been kept strictly under wraps beneath a calm veneer, defying discovery and comprehension. Soon we were again left some distance behind. We watched them walk into the circle of light projected by the florescent lights of the store. This time they came to a stop, standing there, still unspeaking. The man appeared to be trying to tug at the woman, but she again drew away imperceptibly. Under the light of the store, her cheongsam appeared drab and old, the floral patterns already worn thin and the sweat-marinated fabric limply draped on her frame. She raised her hands to cover her face, as if she were crying. But when she let her hands drop at our approach, we had a front and center view of her face and it was serene and composed. Now they gave the impression of two strangers standing in their respective corners, covering up something or feigning something. Strangely the two clerks in the store noticed nothing unusual, but continued their desultory conversation, their voices echoing in the deserted store. A couple of popsicle wrappers had floated down to the floor, crawling along in fits and starts.

They appeared to be in a deadlock, with each side standing its ground. We never saw the man's face with any clarity, partly because he did not cut as striking a figure as the woman. But we could distinctly feel that he exercised a power akin to control over her. The woman was apparently in fear of him. He stood with his back to the light at the edge of the circle of light, very sure of himself. It must be very late now, but there was no moon, much less any stars. The Chinese parasol trees seemed to loom larger, as if growth was accelerated in this humid greenhouse of a night. The couple walked out of the circle of light and passed in front of us. We also turned back. The secret enclave between mother and her colleague seemed interminable and it seemed the movie *Jie Zhenguo* would never be shown that night. They walked ahead of us, one on the sidewalk, the other outside the curb. Then all of a sudden the man slapped the woman in the face. This time there was no mistake about it. We halted in horror, our hearts racing wildly. A show had been staged right before our eyes and yet we did not have a clue about the story. Horror was the only emotion we felt. This drama had a dubious quality: shadowy, turbid and somewhat lurid, and it was close to the denouement. The end was in sight. The woman did not utter a sound after the blow. The two remained mute from beginning to end. There was not a word exchanged, as befitted the conclusive part of the drama: With the mystery unraveled and the reasons teased out, there was no longer need for spoken lines. They looked nonchalant, as if they had been fully prepared for what might happen. They had been tempered and perfected in convoluted plot lines; they were full of complexities. We stood on the sidewalk, shaken, not knowing whether to continue to follow them or turn away. That circle of light was incandescent to an unnatural degree, and a little terrifying. In our hesitation we finally heard mother's voice calling us. It came over the viscid air, laboring, step by halting step, a voice at once familiar and alien. We broke into a run toward the voice.

A Nuptial Banquet

A drizzle was falling. It was a spring rain. A wedding was shortly to take place in Xiaogangshang (literally "on the hillock"). Already that morning someone was sent to the adjacent Daliu hamlet with invitations. These were to be delivered to the educated youth. Xiaogangshang was a small village with only one production team. In contrast Daliu hamlet had seven. Xiaobao hamlet, Daliu's neighbor on the other side, had the ninth team. The nine production teams made up the production brigade called the Daliu Brigade. The educated youths assigned to the locality had been mostly sent to the production teams in Daliu hamlet. Prevented by the rain from going out into the field, they sat inside the door looking dazedly at the barren field outside. The bridegroom was a teacher with a high school diploma who was no longer young at 26, in fact, well past the local marrying age. The delay could be attributed to his early insistence on picking a perfect bride, followed by his demand, once a candidate was decided on, for a reasonable period of dating and getting acquainted, which added to the delay. He had an oblong face, thick eyebrows, big eyes, and a square chin with a slight dimple in the middle. He had a mouth that had some resemblance to what the locals called "mama mouth," although not exactly typical of it, which had the effect of making him smile like a child. He had a younger sister with a similar physiognomy. In contrast to their emaciated widowed mother, who lived with them, both brother and sister were strongly built and enjoyed robust health, possibly thanks to the genes of the father, who had died early in their life. Both had been well schooled. Their widowed mother said with pride that her son and daughter were the most handsome members of the Daliu Brigade. And now the son was getting married.

There were a total of eleven educated youths here, not a big number. Now only ten were left after the return of one of them to his native town—the chief county town. Ten was an ideal number to fill one banquet table. They were not on particularly familiar terms with the teacher, who lived in Xiaogangshang and never worked in the fields. On the few occasions when they crossed paths on the village road, they would merely nod to each other politely and walk on. The teacher appeared more like a city person than any of the educated youths. He was always well dressed, with a fountain pen in his shirt pocket and a pile of textbooks under his arm. He insisted on wearing dress shoes and socks even in summer. In winter he would sport a camel hair great coat, with the lapels open and his hands in its slant-cut side pockets. Winter or summer he would be seen wearing a green army hat with a visor pushed down to his eyebrows, in the style of the early days of the Cultural Revolution. City youths also liked to wear military hats but mostly in a rakish style, or with the hat worn sideways, or with the top of the hat creased into ridges, a bit like the hats of the Chinese Nationalist troops portrayed in movies, a testament to the dejection of the Red Guards as their movement went into free fall. The reverential way in which he liked to wear his army hat gave away his rustic origin. Another telltale sign that he was a country lad was his reed playing. After school, he would walk on the ridges dividing the rice paddies blowing on a bamboo flute. The lilting melody played on his reed and his leisurely gait evoked an idyllic scene of a shepherd riding home in the gloaming singing a country tune. The elementary school was located in the back of the hamlet, or as the locals would say, "behind the homes," separated from the hamlet by some tilled fields. Its lone-standing row of five rooms, sitting by the main road leading to the chief county town, appeared a little forlorn. Since most of the farm land of the hamlet lay in the southern part, few people ventured this way. Mostly these were people traveling on the main road hurrying toward their destinations. Some walked, some rode on their donkey carts, the bells dangling under the donkey's neck making a crisp jangling sound that carried far. A married female teacher from the school was assigned one of the five rooms. She left every Sunday to join her husband, who lived in the commune. Sometimes she left after class on school days. In her absence, the school felt even more deserted.

The bridegroom had rarely ventured out of his home, much less out of his village to visit Daliu hamlet. The bigger hamlets naturally had a tendency to look down on

the smaller ones, while the lesser hamlets
had their own dignity to uphold. As a
consequence, he could be found either at
the school or at home. His home was a very
old three-room mud hut, low-ceilinged
and dark inside, not easily imaginable as
a place that could produce two such good-
looking kids. He occupied the room at the
eastern end and his widowed mother and
his sister lived in the west room, separated
from his by a living room, with a long
narrow table facing the door, on which sat
a memorial tablet (a shrine) in honor of
his deceased father. His room rarely had
visitors, except for one regular guest, who
came nearly every day after supper. The
two of them would head straight to his
room to chat or to make music, with him
playing the flute and the visitor playing the
erhu (a two-stringed Chinese fiddle). The
visitor, also from Xiaogangshang hamlet,
had attended the same school, but was two
classes lower. As a result of his undesirable
class backgrounds (a rich peasant family),

he was allowed only to work the land and any matchmaking efforts had so far been fruitless although he was well past the local marrying age. This school pal of the bridegroom's was very smart; not only did he play the erhu well but he also composed music. He often asked an educated youth in Daliu hamlet, who had a love for literature, to write lyrics for his songs. That was how his association with the educated youth began. Today it was he who had been sent to the to deliver the invitations to attend his upperclassman's wedding banquet. Because of the rain, he put on a big pair of *maowo* (straw shoes made from rush, lined with feathers, felt fragments, etc.), which were warm and resistant to skids. It was damp and cold from the spring crispness and the rain. It was a cold that penetrated to the bone without one realizing it. He shuffled in his *maowo* to where the educated youth lived. They were scattered all over the place; some roomed in villagers' homes and others lived by themselves. He was

wearing only one layer of clothing and
his face was bright from the freezing cold,
but he remained in good spirits. He said,
smiling, that he would be honored by their
attendance at the wedding. He had a coarse
face because of the exposure to the elements
in his field work; his normally rumpled hair
was now flattened by the rain against his
forehead. He had a trowel-shaped face and
protruding teeth, not exactly good-looking,
but distinctive and far from dull. This
might have been attributable to his free and
open temperament. The look in his eyes,
his speech and his facial expressions always
radiated a self-assurance, composure and
joyousness that were hallmarks of a sunny
disposition. When he smiled, his ear-to-
ear grin instantly brightened up his not
so good-looking face. He spoke the local
dialect, but with a difference, probably due
to his more literate, yet not stilted, and
often witty diction. Another distinctive
feature was perhaps his voice, which was a
little throaty, not hoarse, but deep and full-

bodied and very masculine. All in all he was not without his charm. He was more relaxed and insouciant than his upperclassman because of his self-confidence, although far inferior in circumstances and personal advantages. Now his friend was getting married and he remained unsuccessful in his quest for a bride, having come away empty-handed from numerous arranged meetings with prospective brides.

The educated youths who received the invitations were somewhat mystified. What did the teacher have to do with them? These young people who had settled here from cities across the nation and then scattered out to different production teams gathered to discuss what to do about the invitation. A villager who offered room and board to some of these youths opined that they had to attend, and attend with a cash gift in the standard amount of two yuan per person, although children were not obliged not bring a gift. The owner of the rooming house further explained that although they

were from cities and the teacher was a local
country lad, they has all attended school
and studied and therefore in a sense were
schoolfellows. That's why they were invited.
So the educated youths decided to attend
the wedding feast; the owner of the rooming
house asked his tenant to take his son with
him to the banquet. The boy was about five
or six years old, maybe even younger, but
strode sure-footedly on the muddy road
in his small straw-made *maowo*, his hands
skillfully sheathed in the opposite sleeves
for warmth in the manner of a grown-up,
leading the pack of the stumbling youths
wearing rubber-soled shoes and shielded
by umbrellas. The boy disappeared the
moment they reached their destination. A
group of kids brought by adults attending
the banquet could be seen playing in front
of the house in the drizzle. He was doubtless
among them now, but could hardly be told
apart from the rest because of the gloom
and the rain.

When they went in, the house was

already filled to capacity with guests seated against the walls, the inner room reserved for women and the outer room for male guests, all with their hands in their sleeves, and barely talking to each other. They were all a little awkward and grave-faced, waiting patiently for the feast to start. The educated young, on the other hand, sat facing the door, males and females pressing against each other, contemplating the hectic activity around them. In the yard in front of the house a makeshift tent was rigged with a sheet of oilcloth under which a tabletop was placed for honored guests. Through the oilcloth the gloomy sky took on a yellowed hue. Rips and tears in the oilcloths must have let in pulverized, ice-cold raindrops that fell on faces, causing guests to wince during numerous previous wedding and mourning feasts. The teacher's schoolmate acted as traffic director, running hither and thither in the fine rain, his slender, long limbs rowing and his back hunched. The bridegroom made only an occasional appearance, wearing a new serge uniform under his camel-hair great coat, a red velvet flower in his pocket, and a blue felt hat in place of the usual army hat on his head. His cheeks were unusually flushed. He tried without success to suppress his smile by pressing his lips together tightly, the resulting twitching at the corners of his mouth accentuating his babyish manners. He came out to greet the educated youths, but was called away by his school pal before he could finish his sentence, doubtless for consultation about some detail of the wedding ceremony.

It was hard to guess the time of day because of the gloom, but experience told them it must be past midday. In such rainy weather the locals normally ate two meals a day and were likely hungry now after their first meal of the day. From time to time women could be seen emerging from the house to check the front yard to see if their kids were around or to call them to their side to wait together for the start of the feast. But the kids became restive after sitting for a while and would slip away to roughhouse when the adults were not looking. The landlord's boy who came with the educated youths was different. He had twice come into the house to check if the youth who brought him was still there and went back to play only after making sure. It was now even darker inside the house. Some were already dozing with their chin pressed against their chest, and snoring loudly. Everything in this mud hut was drab, the only exception being the poster with the bright red character *xi* ("happiness") newly pinned on the door of the teacher's bedroom at the eastern end of the house. The guests were dressed up for the occasion: The men donned their felt hats and the women had at least changed out of their usual clothes and had square scarves adorning their heads. Naturally, their shoes were all muddied. Only the gang of youths sitting near the door was sloppily dressed: Most of the educated youth were a listless lot. They made a point

of presenting a dispirited, unkempt face to
the world in protest against life's unfairness
to them. They were badly dressed, but with
a dramatic effect. Thus, one of them wore
a cotton-padded jacket without the unlined
outer guazi that normally covered it, and
the buttons had all fallen off so that he had
to tie an elastic band about his waist to keep
the jacket front closed. Another's glasses
were missing their sides and were tied to
the back of his head with a string. One
had his head shaved. Another hadn't had
a haircut for months and his hair reached
down to the base of his neck. The ladies
were slightly better because they still cared
about how people saw them and refused to
look decrepit, but they had nonetheless the
same dejected air. They had more to worry
about and felt the pressure of their age more
acutely. Already in a sulk on normal days,
they were bound to feel saddened to witness
someone else's wedding. That explained the
rigid, tense, defiant look on their faces. This
group sitting just inside the door brought

to the wedding feast a discordant note.

The wedding banquet could not start because the bride had yet to arrive. It would soon be approaching two in the afternoon. Word came that the bride had been held back by her brothers, who wanted the bridegroom to personally fetch the bride. The bridegroom therefore set out toward Zaolinzi ("Jujube Grove") in the neighboring county, where the bride's family lived. The trip would take half an hour in clement weather, and surely longer in this kind of rain. They must be trying to teach a lesson to the bridegroom, who had dragged his feet by insisting on dating and getting acquainted before the wedding was finally scheduled. Why, keep on dating and getting acquainted! Why the hurry to take the bride now? The bridegroom's school friend sailed in with his arms flailing in a rowing motion from the muddy front yard and said to the educated youths sitting near the door, "You must be hungry! Blame it on the bride!" Then he laughed and went past them. It was his school pal who was getting married! The way he laughed and seemingly enjoyed himself would make one think it was his wedding. When was he going to have his wedding anyway? Sometimes people working in the fields would see him and his rich peasant father from afar on the high embankment and would think they were going to a meeting with a prospective bride. Then word would spread in the evening that the matchmaking attempt fell through again. The rich peasant father was taller than the son, with a ramrod straight posture and a broad chest with a depression along the middle line. In this tall but broad and flat-chested figure, people could immediately recognize the father. The father appeared to have suffered less than the son and therefore did not particularly show his age and was better-looking. He was neatly dressed and urbane in manner. He also seemed to show a modern bent. He was one of those country gentlemen who had seen the world and been influenced by modern ideas. All the same he didn't look as smart as his son.

With the bridegroom having just departed to fetch the bride, it would at least be another two hours before the banquet would start. Most of the guests did not much mind the wait, since they couldn't have worked their land in this rain anyway. But the patience of the educated youth was wearing thin and their legs were getting cramps with the sitting. So they got up, stamping their feet, and went out of the house to look around and stretch their legs. The son of the owner of the rooming house was alarmed when he saw the man who had brought him leaving the house. He called out to him in a loud voice, "Hey, are you leaving before the feast starts?" He was concerned that he'd have to leave with the man because he would have no one to take him home afterwards. The guy replied that they were coming back. Reassured, the kid resumed playing. Xiaogangshang was a small village and most of them had never been there before, or had only passed through it, in a few big strides. Now that they had a chance to take a closer look at it, they were struck by its poverty. There were barely any brick houses, not even half-bricked ones. They were often out of plumb. In the misty rain and the mud, the houses crowding on each other appeared to lean and on the point of collapse. There were few trees and only one well, surrounded by a band of crushed brick, unlike in Daliu hamlet, where the wells had platforms paved with slate slabs. The youths didn't find anything interesting in their promenade through the village and returned to stand in the yard watching the kids play. They overheard some older folks comment that nowadays weddings did not have a festive feel because they no longer featured music bands. Women asked to help with food preparations crammed the kitchen and some spilled into the yard; borrowed bowls and plates filled several crates. Meats and fish had been cut and sliced and dried vermicelli were being soaked and softened in water in a big wooden basin. The widowed mother of the teacher, soon to be a mother-in-law, adorned her hair with a red velvet flower and bustled about unsteadily on her bound feet. Curiously, the teacher's sister was not as brightly dressed as usual and her face wore an offended look. She busied herself with cooking in the kitchen and did not come out to greet the guests. Normally she was a good conversationalist but today she had zipped her lips, as if to show the new sister-in-law who was boss.

It was now late afternoon. The overcast sky opened up a bit in the north, allowing some light to shine through, but it was a twilight kind of light. Reckoning that it was about time, the bridegroom's schoolmate began hanging bands of firecrackers on the trees. With thousands of firecrackers exploded, there were always some unexploded ones that fell down to the ground, which the kids collected and lit with the old folks' long-stemmed smoking pipes. The crackling of these residual firecrackers brought some festive relief to the boredom of waiting. Then came word that the bride was here in a bullock-pulled cart right by the embankment. It was a while before they actually heard the creaking wooden wheels of the cart struggling in the mud. The educated youth went back into the house and sat near the door. Hungry and tired from the waiting, they sat there staring into space, like statues of Buddha. There was a fuss outside but they showed no interest in finding out what it was about. Shaking their legs and staring at the floor in boredom, they waited for the feast to start.

It turned out the fuss was over the ground being too muddy and likely to soil the bride's new shoes, a pair of black velvet shoes with a buckle across the top, as well as her nylon socks with floral patterns. There were demands that the bridegroom carry the bride into the newlyweds' bedroom. After the long wait, the pranksters were having their fun. At first the bride would have none of it, but

under the prodding of the guests, especially
the bridegroom's schoolmate who loudly
enumerated the reasons, the bride finally
agreed to be carried. Once heaved onto
the bridegroom's back the bride snickered
and the crowd roared with laughter. Now
she refused to look up, burying her face in
the groom's back, highlighting her short,
shiny black hair tied into a bun with a red
clip. The boisterous crowd followed the
bridegroom with the bride on his back
into the newlyweds' room to the sound of
exploding firecrackers. The children now
split into two bands. One group entered
the couple's room and rummaged through
the bedding, producing painted red eggs,
peanuts, candies and rolled tobacco.
Another group stayed outside and looked
everywhere for unexploded firecrackers.
The kid brought along by the educated
youth was apparently an old hand. First he
dashed into the couple's room on a treasure
hunt and was richly rewarded; then he went
out of the house at a moment when the

firecracker spectacle was at its climax, with loose, unexploded firecrackers and shreds of paper raining down. He was rewarded again with a bumper crop of firecrackers. Food was now being brought to the tables, lifting the spirits of the guests. The women went out to call in their kids to get ready for the feast. The groom's schoolmate came in again to inform the educated youths that the bride liked a laugh. He was obviously pleased by the bride's laughter. It was like "the painter's finishing touch that added the eyes to an almost finished dragon," instantly giving it life. With that comment he happily went away to attend to some other duty. The wedding banquet finally kicked off.

The landlord's boy was in the house, standing against a leg of the educated youth who brought him here. When the guests were invited to sit at the tables, the boy clung to his side. There were no chairs for the children. The younger ones sat on the laps of adults and the older ones stood against the seated adults. When the food was brought to the tables, there was a tense silence. The air filled with the aroma of the food that was laid out on one table after another. The first course was the "four-happiness" meatballs, followed by braised pork chops with turnip, fish, toufu, vermicelli and Chinese cabbage. The steamed buns were made from wheat flour and there was rice wine on the men's tables. The guests dived into the food and the air filled with the sound of slurping. When a kid looked about, the adult responsible for him would knock him on the head with his chopsticks encouraging him to eat, and the kid would resume eating. The educated youth were seated at a table near the door and well supplied with wine. The kid at their table must have attended many banquets like this. He held his chopsticks with a firm hand and reached for the farthest dish, retrieving a bountiful load of meat and depositing it on his steamed bun with no spillage. He ate well and fast. At this moment not the wildest games could distract him from the food before him. He alone seemed to sweep up at least half the food at the table. The two young women at the table ate a decent amount, probably because they were hungry, but the men were mainly interested in the wine, which they drank while playing a finger-guessing game. The bridegroom, accompanied by his schoolmate, came to the table to drink to their health. They were correct and polite with the groom, who after all was not on close terms with them and who had an air of superiority. But it was different with the schoolmate. They did not let him off so lightly and demanded to be invited soon to his own "happy feast," which was a sore subject for him, but he was no pushover and asked in a retort when they were going to invite him to their "happy feast," which in their case had the double meaning of their transfer out of the countryside, certainly a happy event. With the help of alcohol, they achieved some kind of catharsis, and vented some of their bitterness. But there was no bad blood because no one took it seriously on a festive occasion. So they were able to laugh it off. The groom's schoolmate bent down to add in a whisper, "What do you think about the bride? She really loves to laugh, eh?" He was seriously impressed by that snicker of hers.

The bride stayed in her room, not showing her face again that night. Someone peeked in and found a roomful of people, some from the bride's family who had escorted her here and some from the groom's family. The bride sat far back in the room, with her head bowed and her face covered by her hair. One sensed that she was laughing.

The banquet for which people had waited all day was over in less than half an hour. The food on every table was swept clean and not a crumb or a kernel was left. All the bowls and plates were cleaned out. Those who lived some distance away started leaving. On the educated youths' table, only a few buns were left and some soup, but

the wine was finished off. The educated
youths staggered as they walked, their
speech slurred and their tongues turned
unwieldy. The kerosene lamps were lit in
the house, illuminating the big character
xi ("happiness") on the window. After
carrying the bride into their bedroom, the
groom had not gone back into that room
again for fear that others would tease him
about it. He stayed outside the door to talk
to the guests. When he saw the educated
youth leaving, he accompanied them to the
main road. The kid that came with them,
bloated with food and overexcited with a
day's roughhousing, had collapsed in deep
sleep and had to be carried on the back of
the educated youth who had brought him
to the banquet.

A month later, several of these educated
youths were assigned to a job digging a dry
ditch on the east side. On one of their first
days, while they paused for some rest and
needed to quench their thirst, they thought
of the teacher whose wedding feast they had

recently attended. So they headed to his home. The sun was high and bright in the sky and the trees had turned green again, giving a fresh look to the village of Xiaogangshang. The yard in front of the teacher's three-room mud hut was now enclosed by a fence of dried sorghum stalks. The teacher had a class in school, the sister was working in the field and only the widowed mother and the new daughter-in-law were home. They invited the educated youths into the house, boiled some water for tea and brought out some peanuts, which were still mixed with the dates and red confetti left over from the wedding. This time the educated youths had a good look at the bride. She had a bronzed oval face with flushed cheeks, dark thick eyebrows and an easy, hearty laugh. The water came to a boil. They drank tea, ate peanuts and chatted for a while and took their leave, despite the zealous insistence of the two women that they stay to share their potluck.

The Meeting

A memo came down from the county that a meeting of the "three echelons" was being convened at the county seat. The abbreviated name of this kind of meeting—*san'ganhui*—is short for "meeting of rural cadres at the three levels of the commune, the production brigade and the production team." The well-attended meeting was normally held for a half day, with registration in the morning, meeting in the afternoon and dismissal and departure upon adjournment. Room and board was the responsibility of the participants, who would be issued an allowance for missing one day's work.

Upon receipt of the memo, preparations began at the production brigade for the meeting at the county seat. The composition of the delegation had to be decided upon: ex officio members at the brigade level included its party secretary, deputy secretary, director of women's affairs, the accountant, the militia battalion commander and the branch secretary of the Communist Youth League. Each of the production teams would be represented by its leader and its accountant. Then there were two groups with the same administrative status as the production team, i.e. the elementary school and the educated youth. The elementary school, with a faculty of two, would send its person in charge. Due to the location of the brigade in proximity to a not particularly land-rich but densely populated town, only a small number of educated youth had been assigned to it and they were scattered among the production teams and therefore had not formed collective households with a head of

household to represent them. Some opined
that they should send someone whose work
performance was highly regarded; others
suggested someone with connections, for
example someone whose parents were
chummy with county officials. In the end
they selected someone who was the oldest
among the educated youth and the least
able to express herself, to afford her a
chance to see the world and be seen by the
world, thus bringing closer the eventuality
of her early transfer out of this rustic
hole. The next thing to agree on was who
to bring along to cook for the delegation.
They settled on Sun Xiazi. She was a good
choice, a nice girl, smart and hard-working,
and not given to pettiness. A match was
made the previous year between her and
a man from Mohekou, with the wedding
set for the following year. Her father was
a capable farmer and her mother was
remarkably good at befriending everyone.
She had a brother in the army, stationed in
Jinhua. Her 12-year-old sister was already

earning work points in their production team; the only "non-productive" member was a younger brother. This was a family that managed its finances shrewdly. Even in the fallow season in the beginning of the year they could still afford to have a daily diet of two meals of thin gruel and one of a more solid staple. It was an honest family that never owed money to anybody. So Sun Xiazi got the nod to be the cook attached to the delegation. The next question to be settled was where the cooking should take place. Following past practice it should be done in the home of a cousin of the brigade accountant's mother. The uncle, who had a home in the chief county town, offered the use of his kitchen to participants of the *san'ganhui* and other meetings. He had a heart of gold. Sometimes people from the village came into town for a meeting or on a "propaganda show" tour and dropped by unannounced when he was cooking; he would immediately remove his pot from the stove and cede the kitchen to them as though they were his kin. Since the offer was a standing one, the matter was easily settled. Then they'd need to agree on the time of departure. The consensus was they would leave after brunch. There was no need to leave earlier because the county seat was only 12 kilometers away. They would work in the fields in the morning, wash up and eat brunch before setting off. They would be in town by noon and not worry about lunch, with plenty of time before the start of the meeting. At the adjournment of the meeting they'd go to the accountant's uncle's home to prepare the evening meal. This way they'd get in a half day's work and would not inconvenience the accountant's uncle twice by cooking two meals in his kitchen, which would have meant making more than one trip between the meeting venue—the People's Theater in the north of town—and the home of the accountant's uncle situated in the south of town.

The planning went well. Although it was mostly routine, but some kind of planning was necessary to avoid being thrown off balance by unforeseen glitches.

Sun Xiazi also began planning. She needed to decide what dress and shoes to wear on the day of the meeting. Her designation as a delegation member was a great honor for her father and mother. Sun Xiazi never went to school. All she knew was farming and sewing, and she was very good at both. She was strong and didn't mind hard work; she had a quick mind and was a quick study. But without schooling, she could not shine like Xiao Yingzi of Xiaogangshang, who was active in the propaganda team and the political criticism team, and who would from time to time be summoned to the commune or the county seat to join a performance. Sun Xiazi's paternal aunt was a teacher at the non-state elementary school and had on occasion gone to the commune or the county seat to participate in meetings about education, get teaching materials or escort students to tests. Zhao Lingzi of Zhangjia was even more capable;

she was snapped up by a traditional opera troupe when she attended class in the county town to learn model Beijing opera. She had a trowel-like face and a thrust-out mouth but her eyes were lively. It so happened that the female member of the opera troupe who played the role of Li Tiemei (protagonist in one of the model Beijing opera pieces) was also called "Zhao Ling," although it was her real name, while Zhao Lingzi was a nickname. But who knows; they might have been destined to end up in the same troupe. This impression of fate playing a hand in their convergence was strengthened later by the fact that she was assigned the role of Guilan, the girl who drew away the enemy by pretending to be Li Tiemei, thus leading the enemy off on a false scent. The same Guilan of the famous lines: "Although we are two families separated by a wall, we are like one family!" Sun Xiazi could never hope to compete with those outstanding unmarried women in her little world and the thought of emulating them never even occurred to her, but she did look forward to something out of the ordinary happening in her life. If something unusual took place in the days remaining before her wedding next year, it would be a souvenir worth remembering. At the *san'ganhui* the previous year Da Zhizi of the fourth production team went as cook. She was a nice girl with a good heart, never gossipy, never getting into an argument with anybody and got along with everybody. She got married early in the year. At the *san'ganhui* in the year before that, the practice of bringing a cook had not yet started and the cadres had to cook for themselves. The practice caught on after they found out that other brigades were doing it.

Sun Xiazi finally settled on a plaid cotton jacket in black and yellow crossbars to be worn over a woolen sweater knit from yarn that was part of the betrothal gifts from her future mother-in-law. The yarn weighed at least half a kilogram and was of a bright blue, darker than sky blue and lighter than

sapphire blue. It had to be bought in Bangbu
because you just couldn't find it in the streets
of the county seat. She asked one of the
educated youth in her production team to
teach her how to knit in the Shanghai style,
first making the sleeves, then the collar
and finally putting the pieces together. She
took off her padded cotton pants and put
on a pair of sweat pants left behind by her
brother when he went into the military and
over it she wore a pair of blue khaki pants,
also a gift from her mother-in-law. She made
the cloth shoes herself, which she trimmed
with white cloth edging in imitation of
the Beijing-style shoes sold in the streets,
with the uppers done in clear stitches. This
outfit was a little on the flimsy side in this
early spring season, but no matter, not
even her parents had faulted her for being
"underdressed." Didn't those saleswomen
in the department store of the county town
survive the winter without ever putting on
their padded cotton shoes? After working
in the field in the morning of the meeting,

Sun Xiazi came home and poured some hot water which she kept in the thermos under the stove and washed her face, changed and put a handkerchief and one yuan into her pocket. The one yuan was given to her by her dad out of his year-end bonus. She couldn't very well go to the county town without buying something, although she had nothing particular in mind.

The day before departure, the leader of her production team had delivered the flour for the meal and the sorghum stalks as fuel to her home. A cart was brought around to the courtyard. On it sat a wicker basket containing eggs, preserved ham, a small bottle of peanut oil and a military satchel holding several empty bottles for wine. She loaded the bag of flour and the sorghum stalks and shifted and adjusted the load. Then she cut some leeks from her own garden and placed them in the cart. By this time her dad had gone down to the field, and her mother didn't say anything about the leek. But when she went to the vat

of fermented soybean to get some for the
trip, her mother chided her, You eat that
stuff every day; haven't you had enough
of it? Why don't you eat something better
for a change? You disappoint me. She did
not talk back to her mother but went ahead
and deposited it into one of her younger
brother's enamel bowls, placing a scrap
of paper over it before putting it in the
basket on the cart. She thought to herself,
You think I care to eat at the same table as
those men? When everything was in order,
she began her breakfast. When she was
about to get some gruel from the yellow
basin, her mother stopped her with a cry,
You can't drink that cold stuff. Look in the
pot! She still didn't talk back to her mother.
She was in a good mood today, as if she had
suddenly been transformed into a humbler
person. She lifted the lid off the pot and
found fried rice, fluffy and not mushy. Her
mother had a famous saying: "It's thin gruel
only if you can drink it, and fluffy rice only
if it can be scattered." This was rice that

could be scattered. The kernels of rice did not stick together yet were not tough, but soft and fluffy, a little rough on the tongue but chewy and al dente. By the time Sun Xiazi filled her stomach, it was close to noon; the production team leader climbed up the steps and called out to her that it was time to go.

She went out and at the foot of the steps she found cadres walking by. The brigade party secretary and the militia battalion commander pushed their bicycles along, without mounting them. The village, almost deserted earlier in the morning, suddenly came to life and there was excitement in the air. The production team leader put the harness on the cart and she held one of the side ropes. The cart was not heavy, so they didn't have to strain much, except to make sure it was steady and did not go off to one side. They descended the steps and merged with the group of others going into town to attend the meeting. Although they were all from the same village and, on ordinary days enjoyed joshing with the unmarried girls, today they showed some reserve in front of Sun Xiazi and were more careful with their language. This made Sun Xiazi feel a little awkward, but it actually suited her fine. Somebody came over and offered to pull the cart for her, but she declined. After insisting for a while, the helpful guy gave up and she kept control of the rope. The brigade party secretary and the militia battalion commander who had brought up the rear now hopped on their bicycles and overtook the group, the wheels making a shuddering noise as they rode over the dried ruts left by days of raining. They made a u-turn after having gone far ahead and urged the group to walk more briskly to make sure they would arrive before noon. The group quickened their pace.

The sun was bright, in fact so bright it dazzled the eyes. Although there was a crispness in the wind, they no long felt cold after the long march. Sun Xiazi congratulated herself on having dressed correctly for the weather, for if she had put on padded cotton clothes, she would have been bathed in perspiration by now. The educated youth in the group, with the surname of Li, had been settled here from her city for many years now, and had been through different places before ending up here. She had been looking for a production brigade that offered higher-value work points, better living conditions and had a smaller educated youth population so that she could improve her chances of being hired away when there was a recruitment campaign. But what happened was this "shooting and moving" tactic of hers got her nowhere, for she failed to make a deep impression anywhere and nobody thought of her when there was action. Her peregrinations did not bring much improvement to her life either. Whenever a bonus was distributed, people would say, Xiao Li has not been here long. She is new here, so she should get less; or, Xiao Li may leave soon for another brigade, so let her

get her bonus there! Clearly she had made
a tactical mistake. This showed both that
she was not particularly sharp and that
luck hadn't smiled on her. Or she lost her
judgment in her eagerness to get out of
her long rustic stint. She was chosen as the
representative of the educated youth at the
san'ganhui because they felt sorry for her.

There were two female members in
this group. The director of women's affairs
could not go because she had to breast feed
her baby. The two girls, both unmarried,
spontaneously spent more time together.
Xiao Li was not on the same production
team as Sun Xiazi and was relatively new
here, so they did not know each other
well. As Sun Xiazi got to spend more time
with Li on this trip, she found Xiao Li too
subdued by nature. There is nothing wrong
with taciturnity; some people like to talk
and others are less inclined to talk. But
she never smiled either. Granted there are
those who wear a smile on their face all the
time and there are the stern-faced ones.

But she was like a wooden sculpture, with eyes that didn't seem to move. Halfway to town Sun Xiazi could no longer stand Xiao Li's silence and tried to coax some words out of her. Xiao Li did respond but it was the non-committal kind of response and they failed to establish any meaningful communication. The situation reminded Sun Xiazi of a popular saying of the older generation: "The heart is hidden behind a chest wall," referring to how hard it could be to know another's mind. Now Sun Xiazi began to envy the guys walking ahead of them, all chatter and laughter; it would be much more fun to be in their company. But she couldn't very well abandon Xiao Li. Soon however the dilemma was solved for her as Xiao Li split off to talk to the deputy party secretary and the accountant of the brigade. This surprised Sun Xiazi and set her thinking that perhaps Xiao Li felt as uncomfortable with her as she did with Xiao Li. But she quickly dismissed the matter from her mind. A jovial girl who enjoyed

a good laugh and a good chat, Sun Xiazi
could finally breathe freely after feeling so
constrained for such a long spell. She let
herself go now. She got so elated she gave
the side harness a powerful tug, causing
the production team leader to pull the cart
off balance and the cart to veer to one side.
The team leader cried, What are you doing?
Sun Xiazi gave a laugh without replying.
She energetically dragged the cart forward
and resumed her normal pace only when
she caught up with the guys walking ahead.
Looking back and seeing the team leader
forced to break into an unsteady run, she
couldn't help laughing out loud. The team
leader yelled at her, Sun Xiazi! Stop it!

What were the people at the front of the
group talking so enthusiastically about?
It might not be one single subject but a
haphazard mixture of topics. As they talked,
they soon came into sight of the floodgates
at the south end of the county town. The
family who offered its kitchen for their use
was close to the floodgates. That was where

Sun Xiazi would part with the rest of the group, who would travel on in a northerly direction to the People's Theater at the north end of the town, where the meeting was being held. Sun Xiazi was to proceed alone to the home of the cousin of the brigade accountant's mother. The accountant had given her a detailed description of the location and directions for getting there. At this time his uncle and aunt were most probably not home and she would find only the grandmother with her grandson in the house. She just needed to say she was from Daliu hamlet and they would know. The accountant handed five yuan to Sun Xiazi to buy food and some rice wine, and some deep-fried crullers for the uncle's son as a token of gratitude for the use of their kitchen. Then the group resumed the march toward the floodgates. Now pulling the cart by herself, Sun Xiazi took a road by the floodgates downhill toward her destination at a relaxed pace.

At the base of the floodgates people

were washing their clothes and laying them on the concrete terraces to dry under the fiery sun. Following the directions given by the accountant, Sun Xiazi took a ramp downhill and soon found herself on a level road which led to a group of houses, most of which were enclosed by adobe fence walls. The enclosures crowded on each other, obscuring the rare brick houses from view. The walkways between the enclosed yards were narrow and crooked. In comparison the houses and alleyways of Daliu hamlet were much neater. Sun Xiazi got lost in the maze of alleyways and twice went into the wrong house. In one she found only an old man and no grandmother, so she knew it was not the right house; in another she did find an elderly woman, but the woman said she had no relation in Daliu hamlet. At the third house she tried, there was finally a match. This house had a much smaller yard than the other two. Almost half of the house was taken up by the kitchen, and the other, larger half was partly occupied by a brood of chickens. The interior of the house looked dark from the yard. Sun Xiazi thought to herself, Life in a county town is tough! She set down the cart and stowed it in a corner outside the kitchen, trying her best to keep it out of the way. Then, after telling the old lady where she was going, she went into town with her military satchel full of empty bottles.

It was high noon and the sun beat down on the streets paved with cement, where not a speck of dirt was visible. Kids going home for lunch after noon dismissal walked in the street, with their school-bags on their backs and red kerchiefs around their necks. Watching them Sun Xiazi wondered to herself about what their parents might look like. Her first destination was the department store located in the center of town, a two-story structure thrown up the previous year at the intersection of two major streets. Once in on the ground floor, Sun Xiazi couldn't find her way to the second floor. The floor space was huge, with

display cases all around the periphery of the
store and another rectangle of showcases
in the middle, also very spacious. The
salesgirls sat behind the counters looking
haughtily into space with upturned faces.
Sun Xiazi was almost too intimidated to
approach them. She did a walkthrough self-
consciously, finding others who were doing
the same and who could immediately be
spotted as rural, but official-looking folks.
Sun Xiazi reckoned they must also be here
for the *san'ganhui*. When she was on the
point of leaving, after her walkthrough, she
was surprised by a person who appeared in
a corner seemingly out of nowhere. Taking
a closer look she found a staircase behind
a partition, which led upstairs. Sun Xiazi
realized she could access the store on the
second level by climbing the stairs but her
interest had flagged, so she made her exit.

The street had become quieter and
the sun milder. Sun Xiazi was dressed
perfectly for this kind of weather. She saw
a pig emerge from an alleyway and waddle

across the street. She thought to herself that her pigs were better fed than this, and her self-confidence increased. In a store on one of the major streets she bought some rice wine and a pound of sugared crullers. The crullers fresh out of the deep-fry pot looked so enticing she decided to get a quarter pound of them for her own younger brother. She had to break the one yuan note to buy these items; it was only then that she gave thought to what to get for herself. She needed a straw hat for fieldwork. Right now when she harvested wheat she wore her dad's hat, which was too tall, looking like a big, squat thermos bottle on her head. So she needed to buy one for herself this year. But it was still too early in the season to buy straw hats, so she carefully sorted and put away the change from the one yuan note and left the store.

She sauntered in the street, carrying the items she bought. Songs were played loudly on the wired PA speakers, resounding through the entire street, which was otherwise still very quiet. She felt lonely in the streets of the county town; she didn't see anything interesting going on and began to wonder what the meeting participants were doing and whether the meeting had started. She turned into a side street, and found people selling vegetables at the curb. She bought some *lapi* (sheet jelly made from beans) and a bunch of spinach. Then she saw a fisherman selling small freshwater herring offered at a steep discount because the vendor was in a hurry to get back to his boat. She bought the whole lot, almost a pound of it, for four jiao (one tenth of one yuan). What was left of the change she used to buy soy sauce and vinegar. Now she had everything she needed for cooking. She realized the side street led down to the riverbank, and from where she stood she could see the gleam of the Huai River. No wonder there was an odor in the air. It came from the water of the Huai River.

Her hands were full, carrying all the supplies she had just procured and she was hurrying back to a host of chores she needed to perform as cook. Sun Xiazi became extra careful. The street was full of children; some were students who had eaten lunch at home and were headed back to their afternoon classes. It was probably still early for them, so they were taking their time and playfully chased each other in the street. When some of them crossed her path, she would quickly step aside, muttering that she had things to do. She walked past the department store without pausing and without looking back, with only one thought in her mind: I have things to do! As she walked briskly, the solidly stitched soles of her cloth shoes beating a fast tempo against the cement pavement, she acquired a bounce in her steps and her back straightened imperceptibly. All of a sudden she was marching with the gait of a city woman: brisk, hurried, self-important and confident.

When she came near the floodgates, she suddenly made out what the loud voice coming out of the PA speakers was saying. It was a county official reading from a report from the *san'ganhui* meeting. The same broadcast was fed through the PA system all the way to the squawk box in her home. Her dad would be working in the fields at this moment and her mom would be sewing at home, listening to the broadcast. The thought produced a sense that she was so far from her parents and she had already been away from home for such a long time.

The women doing their washing at the base of the floodgates were by now gone home, leaving the half dried clothes and colored bed sheets lying on the steps, flapping in the wind. She descended the ramp that led to the group of houses, and zigzagged through the maze of alleyways to reach the yard of the relative of the accountant. The grandmother was sitting at the door, pasting layers of fabric together to be used as shoring materials for cloth shoes. In a hammock by her side slept her grandson. Sun Xiazi put away the purchased items and seeing that it was still too early to prepare the meal, she sat down opposite the granny and helped by brushing on the paste and compacting the scraps of fabric glued together. The granny was glad to have someone to talk to and told her one thing after another about the family. Sun Xiazi found out that the granny's son worked as a temp at a kiln; the daughter-in-law did odd jobs on the riverfront and occasionally worked in a food stall in town but at other times stayed home because it was not easy to find work in town. The year before a friend found a job for her son hauling flatbed carts in Bangbu, but both the daughter-in-law and the granny got sick and the thing fell through. If he had taken the job, it would have brought in one yuan a day, said the granny with a regretful tsk tsk. With her weakening sight, the granny produced a piece of shoe shoring that was uneven in thickness and full of bumps where too much paste was applied. In the end Sun Xiazi had to take over the entire process of brushing on the paste, pressing the scraps together and adding more layers of paste and fabric, with the granny relegated to talking and handing over materials required in the process. Soon a well-made piece of shoe shoring was pasted together and by then the sun was low in the western sky, signaling it was time to cook the evening meal.

After giving it some thought Sun Xiazi decided on the following menu for supper: scalded spinach, a *lapi* (sheet jelly made from beans) salad, braised herring and scrambled eggs with smoked ham. There would be noodle soup and baked flat bread too. It would be a sumptuous feast. Once the decision was made she began preparations. The fish and the spinach needed to be washed first. She borrowed a pole and two water buckets from the granny to draw water so that she could fill the tank, which was already low. The granny told her that there was a pump near the end of the alley not far from her home but the water was not fit for drinking and could only be used to wash dishes and vegetables. For potable water she needed to go down to the bank of the Huai River under the floodgates and get it directly from the river. She reckoned it would be a good idea to take everything that needed washing down to the river to wash and, after she was done, bring back two pails of river water. She found a basin, which she held in her hand, and carried two empty pails on her pole, and headed to the riverbank under the floodgates. Once there she found women washing vegetables and rinsing rice on the concrete bank. The water there was clear because there was no earthen bank that would have been likely to muddy the water. Following their example Sun Xiazi scooped up water from the river with the basin and did her washing in it. The used water, dumped on the cement surface behind her, formed a large wet patch but was quickly absorbed. Sun Xiazi realized that life in the county town was indeed a bit different. The fact that these women washed their vegetables here showed that people in the county town ate more fresh cooked vegetables, unlike village folks, who salted away their vegetables in a big vat, which lasted them through the year. No wonder her dad said that the inhabitants of Shanghai routinely had a fresh made dish for breakfast. When her dad said that, her mom would, in a jab at him, add, "Preferably to be taken with a few cups of rice wine!"

When Sun Xiazi returned, the granny was cooking, ahead of time, so that the stove could be freed for her use. Now a little girl was in the house; she had just come home from school. A bundle of twigs lay by the door; she had picked up those twigs on her way home. After replenishing the water tank with the water she'd just carried home Sun Xiazi began slicing the smoked ham and the *lapi* (sheet jelly) and putting them in plates. The granny prepared a potful of *gedatang* (dough drop soup, made from shreds of dough dropped into a boiling soup), the drops of sesame oil added to it filling the house with its aroma. When the granny

wasn't paying attention, Sun Xiazi got out
an egg, cracked it on the rim of the pot and
dumped the yolk into the soup, saying the
egg was for the granny's grandson. She then
went back to kneading and flattening the
dough for making noodles. By the time she
cut the flattened dough into thin strips and
shook them into loose strands, the granny,
her grandson and granddaughter could
already be heard slurping their *gedatang*
in the dark. Although it was already dark
outside, the lights in the house had not
been turned on. Sun Xiazi couldn't bring
herself to turn on any light as long as the
granny did not. Fortunately the walls of the
kitchen were made with sorghum stalks and
she was still able to see by the little natural
light that managed to come in through the
gaps. When she thought it was time to start
cooking, she suddenly realized she had
not brought matches. She was unwilling
to ask the granny for one, not that a match
would greatly indebt her to the granny, but
because she felt that borrowing the kitchen

was already imposing enough on the host and she was loath to trouble them any further. Stoking the ashes in the stove with a poker she found some embers among the soybean stalks used a moment ago by the granny. She collected a few soybean stalks lying on the floor in front of the stove and fed them carefully into the stove, spreading them evenly over the embers. She nudged the embers about and by and by, pouf, the stalks caught fire. She got to her feet and went to get the sorghum stalks she had brought from home. She broke one into several pieces and fed them into the stove. Soon the pot was hot but she was not in a hurry to add water to the pot, but continued to feed more sorghum stalk segments into the stove until the pot bottom was red hot. Then she added a gourdful of water, causing a hissing sound as the water sizzled. The water soon appeared to be boiling but she let it boil for a little while longer before dipping the spinach briefly in it. With the hot water used to scald the spinach she

carefully rinsed the wok in preparation for
frying. The water poured on the hot wok
quickly dried. She then collected a drop of
cooking oil with the spatula and ran a bead
of oil around the sides of the wok to grease
it before pouring half of the remaining oil
in the small bottle into the wok. Having
done that she started beating the eggs with
a pair of chopsticks, raising the yolk, which
seemed to grow on the chopsticks, high
above the bowl until froth formed. She
freed a hand to add segments of sorghum
stalks to the stove. When the oil began
to smoke, she tilted the bowl containing
the beaten egg mixture and moved it in a
circle to drop the mixture into the wok. As
soon as the fluffy egg mixture hit the hot
oil, it puffed up to fill half of the wok; she
threw in bits of smoked ham and stirred
the combined ingredients in the wok. She
found it exhilarating. She had never before
had this kind of freedom to use so much
oil in her cooking. During the Spring
Festival her mother took over cooking

whenever it involved a lot of ingredients because she found Sun Xiazi wasteful with the ingredients. But Sun Xiazi considered herself a good cook. Not only did she make delicious food, she had good timing too. She timed it so that the food was fresh out of the wok when the people started arriving from the meeting, filling the living room. The granny finally turned on a pale bulb, which cast a yellowish, sallow hue on their faces. The granny's son and daughter-in-law were not home yet. The brigade accountant went to a neighbor to borrow a tabletop and placed it alongside the granny's table. Sun Xiazi didn't want to sit at the table and Xiao Li wasn't there because she went home as soon as the meeting was over. It was still so crowded at the expanded table that people's elbows jostled against those sitting next to them.

Some helped Sun Xiazi bring the plates of food and the wine to the table and the meal started with the wine. In the meantime Sun Xiazi began sticking flat rounds of dough to the side of the wok to make pancakes. She poured the last of the oil into the wok, barely enough to cover the interior of the wok with a thin coat of oil. Then she put in the small breaded herring to fry until browned and a little burnt before adding chopped scallion, Chinese cabbage, red pepper, Sichuan pepper, soy sauce and salt and half a gourd of water. She let it simmer, mindful of the old culinary wisdom often quoted by her mother that fish needs to simmer even more than bean curd. The dough used for making pot-sticking pancakes was made deliberately looser and more watery. The dough patties were meant to be pressed with one's palm into the side of the wok. This required skill because it had to be done evenly and with the palm applying the right pressure. If the dough was not pressed hard enough the pancake would fall off the side into the bottom of the wok. On the other hand if the pressure was too great, the pancake would become tough and less pleasing to the palate. A good kneading technique was also essential. This time Sun

Xiazi kneaded the dough perfectly, not too watery and not too tough. She stuck the pancake patties along the wok's side evenly and fed sorghum stalks into the stove when necessary to keep the fire going nicely. She made efficient use of the sorghum stalks and she reckoned there would be enough left for the granny's family to use.

After transferring the fried herring into a plate and taking out the pancakes, she started making a second lot. It was then that she saw a shadow walk by in the dark outside, shuffling along with a bunch of vegetables in hand, and appearing exhausted. When she heard the person greet the people in the house, she realized it was the daughter-in-law, the brigade accountant's aunt, just back from work. The group invited her to share their supper but she declined and they did not insist. After a while Sun Xiazi saw her take a stool out into the yard, where she sat down and began drinking from a bowl of gedatang soup. She swallowed it in large gulps, hungrily but without relish, as though it was a duty she had to perform. Her man was not yet back from work.

Inside the house the people sitting at the table, warmed by the alcohol they imbibed, had started a finger guessing game. After working non-stop in the kitchen all this while, curiously, Sun Xiazi did not feel hungry. She was much concerned about the granny's son, who was not yet home at this late hour. But his folks seemed unconcerned, as if it was something they were used to. This was probably the way of the town people. She was waiting for the end of the drinking to start making the noodle soup. She covered the fire with ash, and walked alone to the gate of the front yard. Even with the lights in the surrounding houses turned on it was still very dark outside. The floodgates now appeared very close, looming large over the cluster of houses. There were lights on the floodgates, but they were too high up to reach this far. There was no moon to alleviate the darkness. Gazing at the dark silhouettes of the squat houses, she felt a

sense of melancholy. She was not feeling
sorry for herself but for others, so the
sadness had a good feeling. Another figure
moved in the dark. This time it had to be
the son of the granny! But it turned out to
be a woman. Taking a few steps toward the
form she recognized Xiao Li.

She was pleased to see Xiao Li at this
moment. She said, Xiao Li! I thought you
weren't coming back tonight. Xiao Li had
said it was out of the question because she
had to work tomorrow. The two went into
the yard. The people at the table were so
caught up in their drinking that nobody
noticed Xiao Li's arrival and therefore
nobody invited her to the table. Xiao Li told
Sun Xiazi that she had already eaten and
followed the her into the kitchen, where she
sat down. Sun Xiazi sprinkled some flour
on the freshly made noodles which she had
placed in a shallow container and drew
them up off the bottom of the container a
few times to prevent them from sticking
together. Suddenly Sun Xiazi felt a chill.

After sweating profusely in the kitchen she had gone out into the night air and must have caught the chill from the wind. She bent low to add fragments of sorghum stalks to keep the embers burning and sat down against the side of the stove. Before she knew it she had fallen asleep. She didn't know how long she slept. By the time she woke up, she sensed a weight against her shoulder. It was Xiao Li, who had fallen asleep on her shoulder. She turned to look at Xiao Li but couldn't see her face clearly. What difference would it make if she could make out her features? It would be the same wooden face. With the wooden face pressed against her shoulder, she thought of how Xiao Li had been moving heaven and earth to find a better place and a better life. Look where she has got herself and what kind of life she had! She felt sorry for her and kept still so that Xiao Li wouldn't be disturbed in her sleep. There was no need to wake her up just yet since the guys were still drinking anyway. Those men lost all sense of time

once they started drinking. The granny's
son surely must be home by now?

Xiao Hong of the Village of Huayuan

From hamlet to hamlet, even if only a few kilometers apart, the change in mores is considerable. Each has its own way of life in a micro-environment closed to outside influence. When an inhabitant of one hamlet visits another, he tends to find fault with everything and is struck by the oddity and outlandishness of what he observes. He tends to minimize even the merits of a village because it is not his own and he simply feels put off by what he sees. This bias arises because life in a village exercises a powerful grip on its inhabitants. Before you know it you are already assimilated to its ways as if you had lived there a hundred years.

We lived at the time in Daliu hamlet, seven kilometers from Huayuan ("the Garden") hamlet. To go to the seat of the commune from where we lived, we'd first pass through Xiaogangshang ("On the Hillock"), then Jin'gangzui ("Diamond Mouth"), Jiagou ("the Gulch"), Fengjing ("Well of the Feng Clan") and finally Huayuan ("the Garden"). This gives you an idea of how dense the population is in these parts. Beyond Huayuan lies Toupu ("Main Store"); further away is Toupuji ("Fair of the Main Store"), where the offices of the commune were located. But the village fair there was not as prosperous as some of the other fairs in that part of the country, consisting of one unpaved street, lined by a few mud houses. Business was slack even on a village fair day, when most people would choose to spend

their day in the streets of the chief county
town. Ours was a commune situated on
the outskirts of town. To reach downtown,
people had to pass through our hamlet. To
pass through our hamlet they'd need to go
through Baozhuang, Xiaoji, Dafangzhuang,
Xiaofangzhuang and Caiyuan to reach the
foot of the floodgates, where downtown
starts. It's an eight-kilometer trip. Our
hamlet, seven kilometers closer than
Huayuan to the county town, was already
much more open in its ways. It boasted
quite a number of inhabitants who had
seen the world, and who had received an
education. Moreover, you were likely to run
into expatriates of Daliu hamlet everywhere
you went: a vendor of dates at a country
fair, a performer in the County Traditional
Opera Troupe, a director or an official in
one of the commune offices or a military
man in Jinhua of Zhejiang Province. There
was even a Daliu staff member at Shanghai
First Medical College Hospital. When the
commune organized a performance tour

through its jurisdiction in a propaganda campaign the troupe members were drawn from the propaganda teams of two production brigades: one from Daliu and the other from Huayuan.

Huayuan is a curious name, for such contemporary-sounding place names are uncommon here. The farmland in Huayuan is average farmland and the village is as impoverished and land-poor as other average villages. Its houses are mostly constructed with sun-dried mud bricks and its per capita arable land area is lower than average. A strange place to be called "garden." The hamlets are not randomly named. Thus, the hamlet of "Fengjing" got its name because it had a preponderance of households surnamed Feng and it boasted a renowned freshwater well (*jing*). Xiaogangshang is so called because it is situated atop a hillock (*xiao gang*); because of an abundance of rivers and creeks, hamlets have been built on low hills. Pioneer settlers would move in first and later a hamlet would be established on the hill. The name of Xiaogangshang derived from the fact that it is a small village perched on a lone hill. These names more or less reveal some distinguishing mark of the hamlet. Some villages have distinctive features that do not show in their names. For example Dafangzhuang and Xiaofangzhuang are two Muslim hamlets known for their mean dogs. When a stranger approaches one of these villages, a dog will start barking and immediately all the dogs of the hamlet will join in the chorus, causing the traveler to walk briskly away from the village. But Huayuan truly does not have any remarkable feature to speak of and even its curious name leaves most people indifferent. I once wondered if the name had originated from Huayuankou of Henan Province. Could the inhabitants of the hamlet be refugees fleeing the flood in the years when Chiang Kai-shek, the Nationalist leader, had the dyke at Huayuankou deliberately breached, causing the Yellow River to overflow its banks thus barring the advance of Japanese troops? Some of the refugees could have fled to Zhengzhou, walked on to south Xuzhou along the railroad tracks and headed southeast to end up here, settled down and given their new settlement an old name: Huayuan. This would be a plausible supposition, but I never broached the subject with the inhabitants, knowing the people in these parts are normally reluctant to admit to being uprooted migrants.

Had it not been for the formation of the commune propaganda troupe, we would never have met and known people from Huayuan. It was only natural that the commune had chosen the propaganda team of our hamlet. As previously mentioned, there were a large number of people in our hamlet who had received a higher education. They had versatile talents and many excelled in singing and in playing all kinds of musical instruments. The minimum education level in our propaganda team was higher than primary school. There was also an educated youth from Bangbu and one from Shanghai, who performed, in popular city styles, songs, dances, *kuaiban* (folk storytelling accompanied by bamboo clappers), *sanjuban* (three-and-a-half-sentence ballads) and arias of model revolutionary Beijing opera. The Huayuan propaganda team was picked because it had in its repertory a Sizhou opera (a local opera popular in the Huai River area).

Although the two teams were merged to form the commune propaganda troupe, we kept our distance from each other. On the road, they would always walk half a kilometer ahead of us, so that when we arrived at the destination, they would already be preparing the stage, putting out the instruments and props and changing into their stage garb and making up their faces. That was where we differed: Unlike them, we did not wear makeup for the stage. They applied a kind of grease paint to make their faces look like masks of a red hue with a purple tinge. They had a female part played

by a man, with the eyebrows penciled very
dark and very long and a red dot painted in
the middle of the lips to indicate a mouth
as mignon as a "cherry." He cut a grotesque
figure dressed in an upper garment with a
side lapel, a colored handkerchief tied on
top of his head and trouser legs tied with
ribbons, dancing, energetically twisting
his hips; for all his pains not looking any
less like a man. Although this was on the
outskirts of town, there was often no
electricity and the stage would be weakly
illuminated by two hurricane lamps. When
we entered or exited the stage in the weak
light, sometimes we'd run into purple-faced
performers from Huayuan, who flashed
their white teeth, making the pouches on
their faces bulge. They were smiling at us!
It was a frightening smile, but, strangely
enough, not without a certain friendliness
too. They were on the whole older than
all of us. We were student types, who were
more civil; they, on the other hand, were
country folks through and through. One

wondered how they had learned to sing traditional opera.

After the performance, we would clean up the place, pack and go our separate ways to find room and board. We never ate, slept or chatted together. On our part it was a sense of superiority that kept us aloof. We were proud of being from a big, prosperous village and of having an education; they kept their distance for the reverse reasons. On several occasions the propaganda teams from the two hamlets were lodged close to each other, and had to use the same stove. On one such occasion the Huayuan team decided to let us have sole use of the stove. In the darkness we could see that they had rigged a simple stove with a few bricks in a nearby field. Two sorghum stalks sticking out of the opening of the stove were burning slowly; the flames flickered quietly, a wisp of smoke spiraling up and blowing away. The young woman cooking for their team kneaded dough sitting on her haunches, her body bobbing. A finger-guessing game

could be heard going on inside their lodging
as they drank, but they were not making a lot
of noise. The civilized drinking and finger-
guessing must have gone on till very late in
the night. The next morning by the time
we started our breakfast they had already
packed and taken to the road, walking in
single file, carrying their bedding on their
backs and a bamboo pole with their eating
and cooking utensils and ingredients (rice,
flour, oil, firewood, etc.) dangling at its two
ends. They were all heavily built, including
the man who played a woman's role. Their
shoulders were slightly stooped and they
walked with their feet pointing outward
and the legs slightly bent at the knees, in
the manner of people used to field labor
and strenuous exertion. In the late morning
we also set off to the sound of our singing.

The short opera piece in their repertory
was a story about a family faced with the
prospect of giving up its private plot to
the commune, a matter that divided the
three generations in the family. It had a

simple plot and only a few arias sung to a monotonous tune, four sentences to a stanza, very straight-forward and with little subtlety or variation. But they took liberties with the arias, sometimes drawing them out to double the standard length. Depending on the circumstances, they prolonged or shortened the singing. When they saw a larger than average audience or were cheered by the crowd, they would ad lib and add lines, which they executed with a crescendo that wouldn't come down. Those playing the stringed instruments in the band tried desperately to catch up with the impromptu passages. The strained singing voices were far from pleasing to the ears. They were uniformly hoarse and coarse. The actor who played a female role sounded equally hoarse and coarse despite his effort at achieving a falsetto effect. It was a voice that instantly gave itself away as belonging to someone whose tired old throat had been ruined by red yam meal, the smoke and fire of tobacco inhaled through a long-stemmed pipe and inferior rice wine. There were eight or nine of them, including a cooking woman, and a young girl, their only female performer, who played the granddaughter Xiao Hong in the story of the family giving up its private plot. Quite possibly it was her own name and the granddaughter in the opera was named after the actor. Either way, everybody in their team called her Xiao Hong.

Xiao Hong was about 12 years old, and had a round face with a strikingly white complexion uncommon among country folks in these parts. The fair-skinned people found in these parts had the so-called "sun-bleached white faces," faces that got whiter when exposed to the sun. But such faces were dry and seemingly skinless. Xiao Hong's face, on the other hand, was succulent, smooth and finely-textured. It was so white it shined. If one examined her closely, one would have to admit that Xiao Hong was not a striking beauty. There were plenty of local women who were quite good-looking, but in a very different way. Xiao Hong made a striking impression with her rosy lips and white teeth, her pitch black eyes and eyebrows. She had a full head of black hair with a bobbed hairstyle with bangs, a style not only uncommon in the village but also rare in the streets of the chief county town. She dressed unconventionally too, wearing a light sweater over her cotton-padded jacket, like some male students in city streets. But she was definitely no student. She didn't behave like a student. Students are often more fashionable. While she had a fashionable hairstyle and way of dressing, she did not flaunt it. She was sprightly but not in the way the village kids were. She had some winsome mannerisms and could perform acts that village kids would have a hard time imitating. For example she could dangle in the air with one hand gripping a bough and make her body swing like a pendulum describing an arc. Performing this act, she looked more like a city girl, but not as spontaneous. On stage she knew how to let herself go, and unlike the other members of her team she never applied the beet-colored pigment to her face, and in a perverse way, her bare face looked less real on the stage full of purple masks.

Compared to her peers in the village, she was clearly not as sophisticated in the ways of the world. Maybe she only looked 12 but was in fact younger. Even if she was 12, she was taller and physically better developed than most village kids of that age. Sometimes she would wear an innocent, artless expression, for instance, when, on numerous occasions, she came over to where our team stayed and poked her head in to watch us eat, talk, banter and rehearse. For some reason members of our team felt irritated by her. When she stuck her head in, they would stop talking and look at her with a frown. She did not avert her eyes but stared right back at them, a hand on the door frame. She had a curious way of holding on to the door frame, just like a young child would do, but then maybe she did it in a more conscious way, and might not have been as innocent as we imagined. It was wrong to totally deny her innocence. She did have an innocent look, a look that was incongruent with her alleged age of 12. Twelve-year-olds in the village, especially those who had a rough life, would almost behave like a semi-adult at that age. She had an almost baby-like way of staring fixedly into others' eyes, with her pitch-black eyes opened wide and fearless. Members of our team did not tease her as they would a kid, nor did they shoo her away. But they made no secret of their resentment of her. Frankly it was a resentment more properly directed at a grown woman and not at a child. On one occasion she was running in our direction—it was a curious, flamboyant way of running, joyous and bouncy, that only city kids were capable of. But as she ran, her legs slightly bent, her body leaning slightly backward, and her steps minced, her gait was more like that of a grown woman. In the middle of her run she came to an abrupt stop and cried, "Oh, I forgot to put on my facial cream!" With that she produced a pot of facial cream from her pocket, unscrewed its cap, dug out a glob and applied it on her face. We watched the whole sequence of her movements. Finally a young man on our team said disgustedly, "Look how unseemly she is!"

It was an uncomplimentary remark but was more or less on target. Xiao Hong's behavior did sometimes border on the indecorous.

Strange to say, but whenever she began to get on our nerves, someone on her team would shout, Xiao Hong, come back here, as if they knew we were vexed by her. It was obvious that they loved her dearly. It was not the doting, pampering kind of love; it was more than that. They were a laconic lot, clumsy in speech. Bantering was kept to a minimum among them so that a convivial atmosphere was more the exception than the rule. There was no outward exhibition of their love for Xiao Hong, but you got a clear sense that they were very protective of her. They could immediately sense others' (for example, our) resentment of her and become very sensitive. So they were quick to call her back. But otherwise they pretty much gave her free rein and did not try to unduly restrain her. Immersed in a loving environment, she, like all spoiled kids, was less sensitive to how others felt about her and believed she would be treated by everybody as she was by her own people. She couldn't tell hospitality from hostility. So when she was greeted by the irritated look of people on our team, she understandably met it headlong, unflinching and unfazed.

Sometimes the production brigade for whom we performed on one of our tours would offer us a meal, which would bring our two teams together in the same room. Local custom required that men and women were seated separately and the two female members of their team—the cook and Xiao Hong—would be assigned to share a table with our female members. The two of them sat decorously at one side of the table, like relatives of their tablemates. The cook, obviously a capable woman from their village, was reserved but not nervous, exchanging occasional pleasantries with the others. While showing respect for our side, she gave an impression of considering herself equally qualified to be at the table. Xiao Hong, on the other hand, was quieter than usual, her vivacity now put away, her watchful eyes scanning the table warily. She seemed to have come to a sudden realization that she was not particularly welcome there. It was triggered by a feminine sensitivity and clear-headedness toward members of her own sex. People tend to take members of the opposite sex for granted and are less attentive to their sensibilities, and Xiao Hong was very much a girl who had grown up surrounded by males. She now appeared to have lost her appetite and all interest in the food before her. The cook had heaped omelet and deep-fried tofu on her bowl of gruel but she managed only a few bites, with the utmost reluctance. It was only when people came to their table with their cups of wine to drink a toast that she finally perked up, the familiar gleam returning to her eyes. Picking up her cup of wine, she downed its content with a jerk of her head backwards and a smacking of her lips, just like a grown-up woman well versed in the art of drinking and toasting. She held her wine cup with the little finger sticking out and slightly trembling; after drinking up the content, she tilted the cup toward whoever proposed the toast to show not a drop was left in it. This obviously provoked greater enthusiasm in the toaster, who would demand to have another drink with her. She obliged gladly, saying "I'll drink up if you do," or "I'll drink up; you drink as you please." After a few drinks her face took on a heightened color and a seductive look, with, as the Chinese say, "a face rosy as a peach blossom" and "eyes that twinkle like stars." So it appeared that she was no stranger to drinking and toasting;

and she had a touch of the *renlaifeng*"—the
excitement of children in adult company.
Several times the cook tried to get her out
of the "duel of toasts," but she refused to
be rescued, and blithely drank away. The
men on her team turned to look at her, with
mixed expressions, worried that she had
had too much to drink but also unwilling to
spoil her fun. They only turned their heads
back with relief when the boisterous crowd
proposing toasts finally moved away and
left her alone. As if to assuage their concern
she said, "I'm fine," before sitting down. The
cook urged her to eat some food—buns and
gruel—but she ignored her and swiveled
about to survey the surrounding, feeling
a little neglected now that no one was
proposing toasts to her. A man on their team
left his table to come over and nudged the
cook with his elbow, whispering something
into her ear, probably urging her to keep
Xiao Hong out of trouble. The woman said
with a laugh, "All right. I know." It was a
while before Xiao Hong settled down.

As the meal went on, most of the guests became inebriated to varying degree. A man on our team rose to his feet and staggered toward the ladies' table, clearly intent on proposing a toast to Xiao Hong. He was cut off half way by a man from the other team, who said, "big brother, let me drink to your health. I'm drinking up, bottoms up! You drink as you please, big brother!" The man, who was older than our man, called the latter "big brother" to please him. Our man, full of arrogance and emboldened by drink, pushed the interceptor away unceremoniously and kept on coming. Another man from their team left their table to intervene. Someone from our side got to his feet and they got into a tangle between the tables, with one side trying to stop our man from coming to this table and the other side insisting that he be allowed to do so. Our people became increasingly uncivil and uncivilized in manner and in words, while the other group continued to mask their own absolutely unyielding stance

under a façade of smiling deference. A last
quarter moon now illuminated the space in
front of the brigade headquarters, where
the banquet was held, showing clearly the
residual purple paint, only partially washed
off, on their faces, more evident behind the
ears and at the side of their noses, presenting
a sight at once terrifying and comical. They
tried to appease us, wearing this residual
makeup and strained smiles and slightly
bending at the waist. To show their sincerity
in toasting the "big brothers," they took
turns drinking toasts. Jostled by people
from our team, the cups in their hands were
knocked askew and spilled their content on
their hands and sleeves. The tussle finally
died down, and people returned to their
respective tables to continue the feast. In
the nature of things, alcohol-induced brawls
come and go quickly. One moment a storm
rises out of nowhere and the next moment
the guns fall silent and peace returns.

For the duration of the tussle, Xiao Hong
lay drowsy-eyed in the lap of the cook half

asleep, half listening to the adults' verbal
exchanges. For better or for worse, the
tense atmosphere eased considerably in the
aftermath of the commotion. The female
members of our team asked the cook about
Xiao Hong's family. The woman, who
cradled Xiao Hong like a baby, said with a
smile, there is a mother in the house. Our
girls asked, what about the father? Had her
family been forcefully sent down from the
town? To these questions, the woman
responded with a silent smile. And we had
to leave it at that.

The next day everybody got up later
than usual, when the sun was already a
third way up the sky, casting long shadows
on the ground. They were, as usual, an hour
ahead of us, and already getting ready to
move on. Having crossed swords the night
before, they felt familiar enough to say
good morning to us and said they would see
us about noon at the next stop. They spoke
loudly, their rough, weather-beaten faces
breaking into a smile. Rain fell sometime in

the night, muddying the road. With baggage on their backs, they walked resolutely into the mud, their feet turned outward and their bodies rolling slightly from side to side. Xiao Hong, holding on to the cook's arm, also walked with a rolling motion, her feet turned outward. She was very good at walking in the mud, landing her feet softly and lifting them softly. As she did so, her hips swayed and the colorful satchel with a water lily pattern slung across her shoulder swayed with the motion. From the way that she knew how to walk in the mud, one would think she was a village kid, but the manner in which she did it, and the way that she held on to someone's arm when she did it, led one to think otherwise.

Stories by Contemporary Writers from Shanghai

The Little Restaurant
Wang Anyi

A Pair of Jade Frogs
Ye Xin

Forty Roses
Sun Yong

Goodbye, Xu Hu!
Zhao Changtian

Vicissitudes of Life
Wang Xiaoying

The Elephant
Chen Cun

Folk Song
Li Xiao

The Messenger's Letter
Sun Ganlu

Ah, Blue Bird
Lu Xing'er

His One and Only
Wang Xiaoyu

When a Baby Is Born
Cheng Naishan

Dissipation
Tang Ying